THIS BOOK

BELONGS TO

Tik-Tok of Oz

Oz Titles in the
Books of Wonder Series

∽○∾

BY L. FRANK BAUM

The Wonderful Wizard of Oz
with illustrations by W. W. Denslow

ILLUSTRATED BY JOHN R. NEILL

The Marvelous Land of Oz · *Ozma of Oz*
Dorothy and the Wizard in Oz · *The Road to Oz* · *The Emerald City of Oz*
The Patchwork Girl of Oz · *Tik-Tok of Oz*
The Scarecrow of Oz · *Rinkitink in Oz* · *The Lost Princess of Oz*
The Tin Woodman of Oz
The Magic of Oz · *Glinda of Oz* · *Little Wizard Stories of Oz*

BY ROGER S. BAUM

Dorothy of Oz
with illustrations by Elizabeth Miles

∾꧁∽

Oz: The Hundredth Anniversary Celebration
edited by Peter Glassman
with art and text in appreciation of Oz
by thirty favorite artists and writers

∾꧁∽

If you enjoy the Oz books and want to know more about Oz,
you may be interested in The Royal Club of Oz. Devoted to America's
favorite fairyland, it is a club for everyone who loves the Oz books.
For free information, please send a first-class stamp to:

The Royal Club of Oz
P.O. Box 714
New York, New York 10011
or call toll free: (800) 207-6968

TIK-TOK OF OZ

BY

L. FRANK BAUM

AUTHOR OF

THE ROAD TO OZ, DOROTHY AND THE WIZARD IN OZ, THE
EMERALD CITY OF OZ, THE LAND OF OZ, OZMA
OF OZ, THE PATCHWORK GIRL OF OZ

ILLUSTRATED BY

JOHN R. NEILL

——

BOOKS OF WONDER
HARPERCOLLINSPUBLISHERS

Special thanks to
Bruce and Gail Crockett, whose
copy of the first edition was used to
re-create the dust jacket.
Editor's note copyright © 1996 by Peter Glassman
All rights reserved. No part of this book may be used
or reproduced in any manner whatsoever without written
permission except in the case of brief quotations
embodied in critical articles and reviews.
Printed in Hong Kong For information
address HarperCollins Children's Books, a division of
HarperCollins Publishers, 1350 Avenue of the Americas,
New York, NY 10019. www.harperchildrens.com
6 7 8 9 10
Library of Congress Catalog Card Number: 95-079594
ISBN: 0-688-13355-X
Books of Wonder is a registered trademark of
Ozma, Inc.
Books of Wonder
16 West Eighteenth Street, New York,
NY 10011
www.booksofwonder.com

To
Louis F. Gottschalk,
whose sweet and dainty melodies
breathe the true spirit of
fairyland,
this book is affectionately dedicated

TO MY READERS

THE very marked success of my last year's fairy book, "The Patchwork Girl of Oz," convinces me that my readers like the Oz stories "best of all," as one little girl wrote me. So here, my dears, is a new Oz story in which is introduced Ann Soforth, the Queen of Oogaboo, whom Tik-Tok assisted in conquering our old acquaintance, the Nome King. It also tells of Betsy Bobbin and how, after many adventures, she finally reached the marvelous Land of Oz.

There is a play called "The Tik-Tok Man of Oz," but it is not like this story of "Tik-Tok of Oz," although some of the adventures recorded in this book, as well as those in several other Oz books, are included in the play. Those who have seen the play and those who have read the other Oz books will find in this story a lot of strange characters and adventures that they have never heard of before.

In the letters I receive from children there has been an urgent appeal for me to write a story that will take Trot and Cap'n Bill to the Land of Oz, where they will meet Dorothy and Ozma. Also they think Button-Bright ought to get acquainted with Ojo the Lucky. As you know, I am obliged to talk these matters over with Dorothy by means of the "wireless," for that is the only way I can communicate with the Land of Oz. When I asked her about this idea, she replied: "Why, haven't you heard?" I said "No." "Well," came the message over the wireless, "I'll tell you all about it, by and by, and then you can make a book of that story for the children to read."

So, if Dorothy keeps her word and I am permitted to write another Oz book, you will probably discover how all these characters came together in the famous Emerald City. Meantime, I want to tell all my little friends—whose numbers are increasing by many thousands every year—that I am very grateful for the favor they have shown my books and for the delightful little letters I am constantly receiving. I am almost sure that I have as many friends among the children of America as any story writer alive; and this, of course, makes me very proud and happy.

L. FRANK BAUM.

"OZCOT"
at HOLLYWOOD
in CALIFORNIA,
1914.

EDITOR'S NOTE

Tik-Tok of Oz has a curious history. When L. Frank Baum decided to write a musical play based on his third Oz book, *Ozma of Oz*, he found that he couldn't use many of the main characters, as he had sold the theatrical rights to them for stage versions of his first two Oz books. So Baum created Betsy Bobbin to replace Dorothy and Queen Ann to replace Ozma, brought in the Shaggy Man and Tik-Tok from his more recent Oz books, and substantially changed the plot. The result was an almost entirely new story, which was successfully presented on the stage as *The Tik-Tok Man of Oz*. Never one to waste a good idea, Baum then rewrote the play into the book you now hold in your hands, and if you look carefully, you'll see it owes its origins to *Ozma of Oz*.   —Peter Glassman

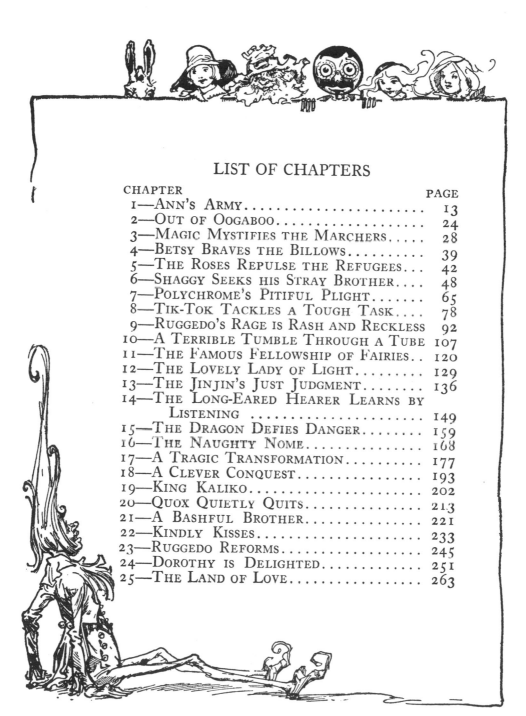

LIST OF CHAPTERS

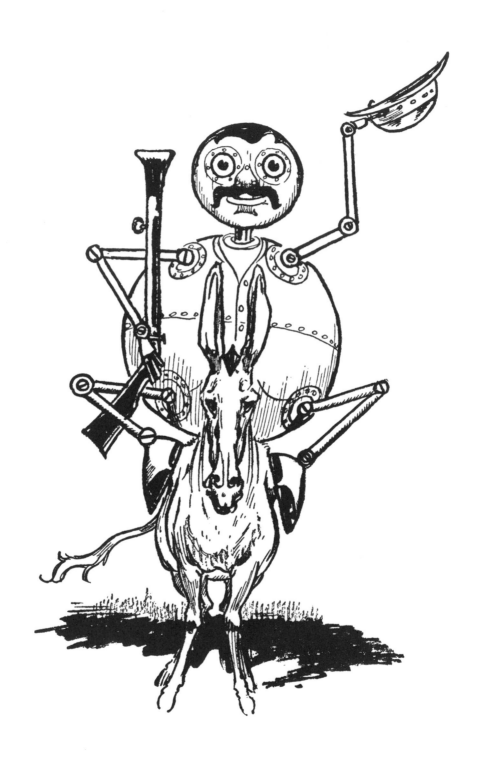

CHAPTER 1

Ann's Army

"I WON'T!" cried Ann; "I won't sweep the floor. It is beneath my dignity."

"Some one must sweep it," replied Ann's younger sister, Salye; "else we shall soon be wading in dust. And you are the eldest, and the head of the family."

"I'm Queen of Oogaboo," said Ann, proudly. "But," she added with a sigh, "my kingdom is the smallest and the poorest in all the Land of Oz."

This was quite true. Away up in the mountains, in a far corner of the beautiful fairyland of Oz, lies a small valley which is named Oogaboo, and in this valley lived a few people who were usually happy and contented and never cared to

13

wander over the mountain pass into the more settled parts of the land. They knew that all of Oz, including their own territory, was ruled by a beautiful Princess named Ozma, who lived in the splendid Emerald City; yet the simple folk of Oogaboo never visited Ozma. They had a royal family of their own—not especially to rule over them, but just as a matter of pride. Ozma permitted the various parts of her country to have their Kings and Queens and Emperors and the like, but all were ruled over by the lovely girl Queen of the Emerald City.

The King of Oogaboo used to be a man named Jol Jemkiph Soforth, who for many years did all the drudgery of deciding disputes and telling his people when to plant cabbages and pickle onions. But the King's wife had a sharp tongue and small respect for the King, her husband; therefore one night King Jol crept over the pass into the Land of Oz and disappeared from Oogaboo for good and all. The Queen waited a few years for him to return and then started in search of him, leaving her eldest daughter, Ann Soforth, to act as Queen.

Now, Ann had not forgotten when her birthday came, for that meant a party and feasting and dancing, but she had quite forgotten how many years the birthdays marked. In a land where people live always, this is not considered a cause for regret, so we may justly say that Queen Ann of Oogaboo was old enough to make jelly—and let it go at that.

Chapter One

But she didn't make jelly, or do any more of the housework than she could help. She was an ambitious woman and constantly resented the fact that her kingdom was so tiny and her people so stupid and unenterprising. Often she wondered what had become of her father and mother, out beyond the pass, in the wonderful Land of Oz, and the fact that they did not return to Oogaboo led Ann to suspect that they had found a better place to live. So, when Salye refused to sweep the floor of the living room in the palace, and Ann would not sweep it, either, she said to her sister:

"I'm going away. This absurd Kingdom of Oogaboo tires me."

"Go, if you want to," answered Salye; "but you are very foolish to leave this place."

"Why?" asked Ann.

"Because in the Land of Oz, which is Ozma's country, you will be a nobody, while here you are a Queen."

"Oh, yes! Queen over eighteen men, twenty-seven women and forty-four children!" returned Ann bitterly.

"Well, there are certainly more people than that in the great Land of Oz," laughed Salye. "Why don't you raise an army and conquer them, and be Queen of all Oz?" she asked, trying to taunt Ann and so to anger her. Then she made a face at her sister and went into the back yard to swing in the hammock.

15

Her jeering words, however, had given Queen Ann an idea. She reflected that Oz was reported to be a peaceful country and Ozma a mere girl who ruled with gentleness to all and was obeyed because her people loved her. Even in Oogaboo the story was told that Ozma's sole army consisted of twenty-seven fine officers, who wore beautiful uniforms but carried no weapons, because there was no one to fight. Once there had been a private soldier, besides the officers, but Ozma had made him a Captain-General and taken away his gun for fear it might accidentally hurt some one.

The more Ann thought about the matter the more she was convinced it would be easy to conquer the Land of Oz and set herself up as Ruler in Ozma's place, if she but had an Army to do it with. Afterward she could go out into the world and conquer other lands, and then perhaps she could find a way to the moon, and conquer that. She had a warlike spirit that preferred trouble to idleness.

It all depended on an Army, Ann decided. She carefully counted in her mind all the men of her kingdom. Yes; there were exactly eighteen of them, all told. That would not make a very big Army, but by surprising Ozma's unarmed officers her men might easily subdue them. "Gentle people are always afraid of those that bluster," Ann told herself. "I don't wish to shed any blood, for that would shock my nerves and I might faint; but if we threaten and flash our weapons I am sure

16

the people of Oz will fall upon their knees before me and surrender."

This argument, which she repeated to herself more than once, finally determined the Queen of Oogaboo to undertake the audacious venture.

"Whatever happens," she reflected, "can make me no more unhappy than my staying shut up in this miserable valley and sweeping floors and quarreling with Sister Salye; so I will venture all, and win what I may."

That very day she started out to organize her Army.

The first man she came to was Jo Apple, so called because he had an apple orchard.

"Jo," said Ann, "I am going to conquer the world, and I want you to join my Army."

"Don't ask me to do such a fool thing, for I must politely refuse Your Majesty," said Jo Apple.

"I have no intention of asking you. I shall command you, as Queen of Oogaboo, to join," said Ann.

"In that case, I suppose I must obey," the man remarked, in a sad voice. "But I pray you to consider that I am a very important citizen, and for that reason am entitled to an office of high rank."

"You shall be a General," promised Ann.

"With gold epaulets and a sword?" he asked.

"Of course," said the Queen.

Then she went to the next man, whose name was Jo Bunn, as he owned an orchard where graham-buns and wheat-buns, in great variety, both hot and cold, grew on the trees.

"Jo," said Ann, "I am going to conquer the world, and I command you to join my Army."

"Impossible!" he exclaimed. "The bun crop has to be picked."

"Let your wife and children do the picking," said Ann.

"But I'm a man of great importance, Your Majesty," he protested.

"For that reason you shall be one of my Generals, and wear a cocked hat with gold braid, and curl your mustaches and clank a long sword," she promised.

So he consented, although sorely against his will, and the Queen walked on to the next cottage. Here lived Jo Cone, so called because the trees in his orchard bore crops of excellent ice-cream cones.

"Jo," said Ann, "I am going to conquer the world, and you must join my Army."

"Excuse me, please," said Jo Cone. "I am a bad fighter. My good wife conquered me years ago, for she can fight better than I. Take her, Your Majesty, instead of me, and I'll bless you for the favor."

"This must be an army of men—fierce, ferocious warriors," declared Ann, looking sternly upon the mild little man.

18

"And you will leave my wife here in Oogaboo?" he asked.

"Yes; and make you a General."

"I'll go," said Jo Cone, and Ann went on to the cottage of Jo Clock, who had an orchard of clock-trees. This man at first insisted that he would not join the army, but Queen Ann's promise to make him a General finally won his consent.

"How many Generals are there in your army?" he asked.

"Four, so far," replied Ann.

"And how big will the army be?" was his next question.

"I intend to make every one of the eighteen men in Oogaboo join it," she said.

"Then four Generals are enough," announced Jo Clock. "I advise you to make the rest of them Colonels."

Ann tried to follow his advice. The next four men she visited—who were Jo Plum, Jo Egg, Jo Banjo and Jo Cheese, named after the trees in their orchards—she made Colonels of her Army; but the fifth one, Jo Nails, said Colonels and Generals were getting to be altogether too common in the Army of Oogaboo and he preferred to be a Major. So Jo Nails, Jo Cake, Jo Ham and Jo Stockings were all four made Majors, while the next four—Jo Sandwich, Jo Padlocks, Jo Sundae and Jo Buttons—were appointed Captains of the Army.

But now Queen Ann was in a quandary. There remained but two other men in all Oogaboo, and if she made these two Lieutenants, while there were four Captains, four Majors, four Colonels and four Generals, there was likely to be jealousy in her army, and perhaps mutiny and desertions.

One of these men, however, was Jo Candy, and he would not go at all. No promises could tempt him, nor could threats move him. He said he must remain at home to harvest his crop of jackson-balls, lemon-drops, bonbons and chocolate-creams. Also he had large fields of crackerjack and buttered pop corn to be mowed and threshed, and he was determined not to disappoint the children of Oogaboo by going away to conquer the world and so let the candy crop spoil.

Finding Jo Candy so obstinate, Queen Ann let him have his own way and continued her journey to the house of the eighteenth and last man in Oogaboo, who was a young fellow named Jo Files. This Files had twelve trees which bore steel files of various sorts; but also he had nine book-trees, on which grew a choice selection of story-books. In case you have never seen books growing upon trees, I will explain that those in Jo Files' orchard were enclosed in broad green husks which, when fully ripe, turned to a deep red color. Then the books were picked and husked and were ready to read. If they were picked too soon, the stories were found to be confused and uninteresting and the spelling bad. However, if allowed to ripen perfectly, the stories were fine reading and the spelling and grammar excellent.

Files freely gave his books to all who wanted them, but the

people of Oogaboo cared little for books and so he had to read most of them himself, before they spoiled. For, as you probably know, as soon as the books were read the words disappeared and the leaves withered and faded—which is the worst fault of all books which grow upon trees.

When Queen Ann spoke to this young man Files, who was both intelligent and ambitious, he said he thought it would be great fun to conquer the world. But he called her attention to the fact that he was far superior to the other men of her army. Therefore, he would not be one of her Generals or Colonels or Majors or Captains, but claimed the honor of being sole Private.

Ann did not like this idea at all.

"I hate to have a Private Soldier in my army," she said; "they're so common. I am told that Princess Ozma once had a private soldier, but she made him her Captain-General, which is good evidence that the private was unnecessary."

"Ozma's army doesn't fight," returned Files; "but your army must fight like fury in order to conquer the world. I have read in my books that it is always the private soldiers who do the fighting, for no officer is ever brave enough to face the foe. Also, it stands to reason that your officers must have some one to command and to issue their orders to; therefore I'll be the one. I long to slash and slay the enemy and become a hero. Then, when we return to Oogaboo, I'll take all the marbles away from the children and melt them up and make a marble statue of myself for all to look upon and admire."

Ann was much pleased with Private Files. He seemed indeed to be such a warrior as she needed in her enterprise, and her hopes of success took a sudden bound when Files told her he knew where a gun-tree grew and would go there at once and pick the ripest and biggest musket the tree bore.

CHAPTER 2

Out of Oogaboo

THREE days later the Grand Army of Oogaboo assembled in the square in front of the royal palace. The sixteen officers were attired in gorgeous uniforms and carried sharp, glittering swords. The Private had picked his gun and, although it was not a very big weapon, Files tried to look fierce and succeeded so well that all his commanding officers were secretly afraid of him.

The women were there, protesting that Queen Ann Soforth had no right to take their husbands and fathers from them; but Ann commanded them to keep silent, and that was the hardest order to obey they had ever received.

The Queen appeared before her Army dressed in an impos-

ing uniform of green, covered with gold braid. She wore a green soldier-cap with a purple plume in it and looked so royal and dignified that everyone in Oogaboo except the Army was glad she was going. The Army was sorry she was not going alone.

"Form ranks!" she cried in her shrill voice.

Salye leaned out of the palace window and laughed.

"I believe your Army can run better than it can fight," she observed.

"Of course," replied General Bunn, proudly. "We're not looking for trouble, you know, but for plunder. The more plunder and the less fighting we get, the better we shall like our work."

"For my part," said Files, "I prefer war and carnage to anything. The only way to become a hero is to conquer, and the story-books all say that the easiest way to conquer is to fight."

"That's the idea, my brave man!" agreed Ann. "To fight is to conquer and to conquer is to secure plunder and to secure plunder is to become a hero. With such noble determination to back me, the world is mine! Good-bye, Salye. When we return we shall be rich and famous. Come, Generals; let us march."

At this the Generals straightened up and threw out their chests. Then they swung their glittering swords in rapid circles and cried to the Colonels:

"For—ward March!"

Then the Colonels shouted to the Majors: "For—ward March!" and the Majors yelled to the Captains: "For—ward March!" and the Captains screamed to the Private:

"For—ward March!"

So Files shouldered his gun and began to march, and all the officers followed after him. Queen Ann came last of all, rejoicing in her noble army and wondering why she had not decided long ago to conquer the world.

In this order the procession marched out of Oogaboo and took the narrow mountain pass which led into the lovely Fairyland of Oz.

CHAPTER 3

Magic Mystifies the Marchers

PRINCESS OZMA was all unaware that the Army of Oogaboo, led by their ambitious Queen, was determined to conquer
her Kingdom. The beautiful girl Ruler of Oz was busy with
the welfare of her subjects and had no time to think of Ann
Soforth and her disloyal plans. But there was one who constantly guarded the peace and happiness of the Land of Oz
and this was the Official Sorceress of the Kingdom, Glinda
the Good.

In her magnificent castle, which stands far north of the
Emerald City where Ozma holds her court, Glinda owns a
wonderful magic Record Book, in which is printed every event
that takes place anywhere, just as soon as it happens.

Chapter Three

The smallest things and the biggest things are all recorded in this book. If a child stamps its foot in anger, Glinda reads about it; if a city burns down, Glinda finds the fact noted in her book.

The Sorceress always reads her Record Book every day, and so it was she knew that Ann Soforth, Queen of Oogaboo, had foolishly assembled an army of sixteen officers and one private soldier, with which she intended to invade and conquer the Land of Oz.

There was no danger but that Ozma, supported by the magic arts of Glinda the Good and the powerful Wizard of Oz —both her firm friends—could easily defeat a far more imposing army than Ann's; but it would be a shame to have the peace of Oz interrupted by any sort of quarreling or fighting. So Glinda did not even mention the matter to Ozma, or to anyone else. She merely went into a great chamber of her castle, known as the Magic Room, where she performed a magical ceremony which caused the mountain pass that led from Oogaboo to make several turns and twists. The result was that when Ann and her army came to the end of the pass they were not in the Land of Oz at all, but in an adjoining territory that was quite distinct from Ozma's domain and separated from Oz by an invisible barrier.

As the Oogaboo people emerged into this country, the pass they had traversed disappeared behind them and it was not likely they would ever find their way back into the valley of Oogaboo. They were greatly puzzled, indeed, by their surroundings and did not know which way to go. None of them had ever visited Oz, so it took them some time to discover they were not in Oz at all, but in an unknown country.

"Never mind," said Ann, trying to conceal her disappointment; "we have started out to conquer the world, and here is part of it. In time, as we pursue our victorious journey, we will doubtless come to Oz; but, until we get there, we may as well conquer whatever land we find ourselves in."

"Have we conquered this place, Your Majesty?" anxiously inquired Major Cake.

"Most certainly," said Ann. "We have met no people, as yet, but when we do, we will inform them that they are our slaves."

"And afterward we will plunder them of all their possessions," added General Apple.

"They may not possess anything," objected Private Files; "but I hope they will fight us, just the same. A peaceful conquest wouldn't be any fun at all."

"Don't worry," said the Queen. "*We* can fight, whether our foes do or not; and perhaps we would find it more comfortable to have the enemy surrender promptly."

It was a barren country and not very pleasant to travel in. Moreover, there was little for them to eat, and as the officers became hungry they became fretful. Many would have deserted had they been able to find their way home, but as the Oogaboo people were now hopelessly lost in a strange country they considered it more safe to keep together than to separate.

Queen Ann's temper, never very agreeable, became sharp and irritable as she and her army tramped over the rocky roads without encountering either people or plunder. She scolded her officers until they became surly, and a few of them were disloyal enough to ask her to hold her tongue. Others began to reproach her for leading them into difficulties and in the space of three unhappy days every man was mourning for his orchard in the pretty valley of Oogaboo.

Files, however, proved a different sort. The more difficulties he encountered the more cheerful he became, and the sighs of the officers were answered by the merry whistle of the Private. His pleasant disposition did much to encourage Queen Ann and before long she consulted the Private Soldier more often than she did his superiors.

It was on the third day of their pilgrimage that they encountered their first adventure. Toward evening the sky was suddenly darkened and Major Nails exclaimed:

"A fog is coming toward us."

"I do not think it is a fog," replied Files, looking with interest at the approaching cloud. "It seems to me more like the breath of a Rak."

"What is a Rak?" asked Ann, looking about fearfully.

"A terrible beast with a horrible appetite," answered the soldier, growing a little paler than usual. "I have never seen a Rak, to be sure, but I have read of them in the story-books that grew in my orchard, and if this is indeed one of those fearful monsters, we are not likely to conquer the world."

Hearing this, the officers became quite worried and gathered closer about their soldier.

"What is the thing like?" asked one.

"The only picture of a Rak that I ever saw in a book was rather blurred," said Files, "because the book was not quite ripe when it was picked. But the creature can fly in the air and run like a deer and swim like a fish. Inside its body is a glowing furnace of fire, and the Rak breathes in air and breathes out smoke, which darkens the sky for miles around, wherever it goes. It is bigger than a hundred men and feeds on any living thing."

The officers now began to groan and to tremble, but Files tried to cheer them, saying:

"It may not be a Rak, after all, that we see approaching us, and you must not forget that we people of Oogaboo, which is part of the fairyland of Oz, cannot be killed."

"Nevertheless," said Captain Buttons, "if the Rak catches us, and chews us up into small pieces, and swallows us—what will happen then?"

Chapter Three

"Then each small piece will still be alive," declared Files.

"I cannot see how that would help us," wailed Colonel Banjo. "A hamburger steak is a hamburger steak, whether it is alive or not!"

"I tell you, this may not be a Rak," persisted Files. "We will know, when the cloud gets nearer, whether it is the breath of a Rak or not. If it has no smell at all, it is probably a fog; but if it has an odor of salt and pepper, it is a Rak and we must prepare for a desperate fight."

They all eyed the dark cloud fearfully. Before long it reached the frightened group and began to envelop them. Every nose sniffed the cloud—and every one detected in it the odor of salt and pepper.

"The Rak!" shouted Private Files, and with a howl of despair the sixteen officers fell to the ground, writhing and moaning in anguish. Queen Ann sat down upon a rock and faced the cloud more bravely, although her heart was beating fast. As for Files, he calmly loaded his gun and stood ready to fight the foe, as a soldier should.

They were now in absolute darkness, for the cloud which covered the sky and the setting sun was black as ink. Then through the gloom appeared two round, glowing balls of red, and Files at once decided these must be the monster's eyes.

He raised his gun, took aim and fired.

There were several bullets in the gun, all gathered from an

excellent bullet-tree in Oogaboo, and they were big and hard. They flew toward the monster and struck it, and with a wild, weird cry the Rak came fluttering down and its huge body fell plump upon the forms of the sixteen officers, who thereupon screamed louder than before.

"Badness me!" moaned the Rak. "See what you've done with that dangerous gun of yours!"

"I can't see," replied Files, "for the cloud formed by your breath darkens my sight!"

"Don't tell me it was an accident," continued the Rak, reproachfully, as it still flapped its wings in a helpless manner. "Don't claim you didn't know the gun was loaded, I beg of you!"

"I don't intend to," replied Files. "Did the bullets hurt you very badly?"

"One has broken my jaw, so that I can't open my mouth. You will notice that my voice sounds rather harsh and husky, because I have to talk with my teeth set close together. Another bullet broke my left wing, so that I can't fly; and still another broke my right leg, so that I can't walk. It was the most careless shot I ever heard of!"

"Can't you manage to lift your body off from my commanding officers?" inquired Files. "From their cries I'm afraid your great weight is crushing them."

"I hope it is," growled the Rak. "I want to crush them, if

possible, for I have a bad disposition. If only I could open my mouth, I'd eat all of you, although my appetite is poorly this warm weather."

With this the Rak began to roll its immense body sidewise, so as to crush the officers more easily; but in doing this it rolled completely off from them and the entire sixteen scrambled to their feet and made off as fast as they could run.

Private Files could not see them go but he knew from the sound of their voices that they had escaped, so he ceased to worry about them.

"Pardon me if I now bid you good-bye," he said to the Rak. "The parting is caused by our desire to continue our journey. If you die, do not blame me, for I was obliged to shoot you as a matter of self-protection."

"I shall not die," answered the monster, "for I bear a charmed life. But I beg you not to leave me!"

"Why not?" asked Files.

"Because my broken jaw will heal in about an hour, and then I shall be able to eat you. My wing will heal in a day and my leg will heal in a week, when I shall be as well as ever. Having shot me, and so caused me all this annoyance, it is only fair and just that you remain here and allow me to eat you as soon as I can open my jaws."

"I beg to differ with you," returned the soldier firmly. "I have made an engagement with Queen Ann of Oogaboo to

36

help her conquer the world, and I cannot break my word for the sake of being eaten by a Rak."

"Oh; that's different," said the monster. "If you've an engagement, don't let me detain you."

So Files felt around in the dark and grasped the hand of the trembling Queen, whom he led away from the flapping, sighing Rak. They stumbled over the stones for a way but presently began to see dimly the path ahead of them, as they got farther and farther away from the dreadful spot where the wounded monster lay.

By and by they reached a little hill and could see the last rays of the sun flooding a pretty valley beyond, for now they had passed beyond the cloudy breath of the Rak. Here were huddled the sixteen officers, still frightened and panting from their run. They had halted only because it was impossible for them to run any farther.

Queen Ann gave them a severe scolding for their cowardice, at the same time praising Files for his courage.

"We are wiser than he, however," muttered General Clock, "for by running away we are now able to assist Your Majesty in conquering the world; whereas, had Files been eaten by the Rak, he would have deserted your Army."

After a brief rest they descended into the valley, and as soon as they were out of sight of the Rak the spirits of the entire party rose quickly. Just at dusk they came to a brook, on the banks of which Queen Ann commanded them to make camp for the night.

Each officer carried in his pocket a tiny white tent. This, when placed upon the ground, quickly grew in size until it was large enough to permit the owner to enter it and sleep within its canvas walls. Files was obliged to carry a knapsack, in which was not only his own tent but an elaborate pavilion for Queen Ann, besides a bed and chair and a magic table. This table, when set upon the ground in Ann's pavilion, became of large size, and in a drawer of the table was contained the Queen's supply of extra clothing, her manicure and toilet articles and other necessary things. The royal bed was the only one in the camp, the officers and private sleeping in hammocks attached to their tent poles.

There was also in the knapsack a flag bearing the royal emblem of Oogaboo, and this flag Files flew upon its staff every night, to show that the country they were in had been conquered by the Queen of Oogaboo. So far, no one but themselves had seen the flag, but Ann was pleased to see it flutter in the breeze and considered herself already a famous conqueror.

CHAPTER 4

Betsy Braves the Billows

THE waves dashed and the lightning flashed and the thunder rolled and the ship struck a rock. Betsy Bobbin was running across the deck and the shock sent her flying through the air until she fell with a splash into the dark blue water. The same shock caught Hank, a thin little, sad-faced mule, and tumbled him also into the sea, far from the ship's side.

When Betsy came up, gasping for breath because the wet plunge had surprised her, she reached out in the dark and grabbed a bunch of hair. At first she thought it was the end of a rope, but presently she heard a dismal "Hee-haw!" and knew she was holding fast to the end of Hank's tail.

Suddenly the sea was lighted up by a vivid glare. The

ship, now in the far distance, caught fire, blew up and sank beneath the waves.

Betsy shuddered at the sight, but just then her eye caught a mass of wreckage floating near her and she let go the mule's tail and seized the rude raft, pulling herself up so that she rode upon it in safety. Hank also saw the raft and swam to it, but he was so clumsy he never would have been able to climb upon it had not Betsy helped him to get aboard.

They had to crowd close together, for their support was only a hatch-cover torn from the ship's deck; but it floated them fairly well and both the girl and the mule knew it would keep them from drowning.

The storm was not over, by any means, when the ship went down. Blinding bolts of lightning shot from cloud to cloud and the clamor of deep thunderclaps echoed far over the sea. The waves tossed the little raft here and there as a child tosses a rubber ball and Betsy had a solemn feeling that for hundreds of watery miles in every direction there was no living thing besides herself and the small donkey.

Perhaps Hank had the same thought, for he gently rubbed his nose against the frightened girl and said "Hee-haw!" in his softest voice, as if to comfort her.

"You'll protect me, Hank dear, won't you?" she cried helplessly, and the mule said "Hee-haw!" again, in tones that meant a promise.

Chapter Four

On board the ship, during the days that preceded the wreck, when the sea was calm, Betsy and Hank had become good friends; so, while the girl might have preferred a more powerful protector in this dreadful emergency, she felt that the mule would do all in a mule's power to guard her safety.

All night they floated, and when the storm had worn itself out and passed away with a few distant growls, and the waves had grown smaller and easier to ride, Betsy stretched herself out on the wet raft and fell asleep.

Hank did not sleep a wink. Perhaps he felt it his duty to guard Betsy. Anyhow, he crouched on the raft beside the tired sleeping girl and watched patiently until the first light of dawn swept over the sea.

The light wakened Betsy Bobbin. She sat up, rubbed her eyes and stared across the water.

"Oh, Hank; there's land ahead!" she exclaimed.

"Hee-haw!" answered Hank in his plaintive voice.

The raft was floating swiftly toward a very beautiful country and as they drew near Betsy could see banks of lovely flowers showing brightly between leafy trees. But no people were to be seen at all.

CHAPTER 5

The Roses Repulse the Refugees

GENTLY the raft grated on the sandy beach. Then Betsy easily waded ashore, the mule following closely behind her. The sun was now shining and the air was warm and laden with the fragrance of roses.

"I'd like some breakfast, Hank," remarked the girl, feeling more cheerful now that she was on dry land; "but we can't eat the flowers, although they do smell mighty good."

"Hee-haw!" replied Hank and trotted up a little pathway to the top of the bank.

Betsy followed and from the eminence looked around her. A little way off stood a splendid big greenhouse, its thousands of crystal panes glittering in the sunlight.

42

Chapter Five

"There ought to be people somewhere 'round," observed Betsy thoughtfully; "gardeners, or somebody. Let's go and see, Hank. I'm getting hungrier ev'ry minute."

So they walked toward the great greenhouse and came to its entrance without meeting with anyone at all. A door stood ajar, so Hank went in first, thinking if there was any danger he could back out and warn his companion. But Betsy was close at his heels and the moment she entered was lost in amazement at the wonderful sight she saw.

The greenhouse was filled with magnificent rosebushes, all growing in big pots. On the central stem of each bush bloomed a splendid Rose, gorgeously colored and deliciously fragrant, and in the center of each Rose was the face of a lovely girl.

As Betsy and Hank entered, the heads of the Roses were drooping and their eyelids were closed in slumber; but the mule was so amazed that he uttered a loud "Hee-haw!" and at the sound of his harsh voice the rose leaves fluttered, the Roses raised their heads and a hundred startled eyes were instantly fixed upon the intruders.

"I—I beg your pardon!" stammered Betsy, blushing and confused.

"O-o-o-h!" cried the Roses, in a sort of sighing chorus; and one of them added: "What a horrid noise!"

"Why, that was only Hank," said Betsy, and as if to prove

43

the truth of her words the mule uttered another loud "Hee-haw!"

At this all the Roses turned on their stems as far as they were able and trembled as if some one were shaking their bushes. A dainty Moss Rose gasped: "Dear me! How dreadfully dreadful!"

"It isn't dreadful at all," said Betsy, somewhat indignant. "When you get used to Hank's voice it will put you to sleep."

The Roses now looked at the mule less fearfully and one of them asked:

"Is that savage beast named Hank?"

"Yes; Hank's my comrade, faithful and true," answered the girl, twining her arms around the little mule's neck and hugging him tight. "Aren't you, Hank?"

Hank could only say in reply: "Hee-haw!" and at his bray the Roses shivered again.

"Please go away!" begged one. "Can't you see you're frightening us out of a week's growth?"

"Go away!" echoed Betsy. "Why, we've no place to go. We've just been wrecked."

"Wrecked?" asked the Roses in a surprised chorus.

"Yes; we were on a big ship and the storm came and wrecked it," explained the girl. "But Hank and I caught hold of a raft and floated ashore to this place, and—we're tired and hungry. What country *is* this, please?"

"This is the Rose Kingdom," replied the Moss Rose, haughtily, "and it is devoted to the culture of the rarest and fairest Roses grown."

"I believe it," said Betsy, admiring the pretty blossoms.

"But only Roses are allowed here," continued a delicate Tea Rose, bending her brows in a frown; "therefore you must go away before the Royal Gardener finds you and casts you back into the sea."

"Oh! Is there a Royal Gardener, then?" inquired Betsy.

"To be sure."

"And is he a Rose, also?"

"Of course not; he's a man—a wonderful man," was the reply.

"Well, I'm not afraid of a man," declared the girl, much relieved, and even as she spoke the Royal Gardener popped into the greenhouse—a spading fork in one hand and a watering pot in the other.

He was a funny little man, dressed in a rose-colored costume, with ribbons at his knees and elbows, and a bunch of ribbons in his hair. His eyes were small and twinkling, his nose sharp and his face puckered and deeply lined.

"O-ho!" he exclaimed, astonished to find strangers in his greenhouse, and when Hank gave a loud bray the Gardener threw the watering pot over the mule's head and danced around with his fork, in such agitation that presently he fell over the handle of the implement and sprawled at full length upon the ground.

Betsy laughed and pulled the watering pot off from Hank's head.   The little mule was angry at the treatment he had received and backed toward the Gardener threateningly.

"Look out for his heels!" called Betsy warningly and the Gardener scrambled to his feet and hastily hid behind the Roses.

"You are breaking the Law!" he shouted, sticking out his head to glare at the girl and the mule.

"What Law?" asked Betsy.

"The Law of the Rose Kingdom.   No strangers are allowed in these domains."

"Not when they're shipwrecked?" she inquired.

"The Law doesn't except shipwrecks," replied the Royal Gardener, and he was about to say more when suddenly there was a crash of glass and a man came tumbling through the roof of the greenhouse and fell plump to the ground.

CHAPTER 6

Shaggy Seeks his Stray Brother

THIS sudden arrival was a queer looking man, dressed all in garments so shaggy that Betsy at first thought he must be some animal. But the stranger ended his fall in a sitting position and then the girl saw it was really a man. He held an apple in his hand, which he had evidently been eating when he fell, and so little was he jarred or flustered by the accident that he continued to munch this apple as he calmly looked around him.

"Good gracious!" exclaimed Betsy, approaching him. "Who *are* you, and where did you come from?"

"Me? Oh, I'm Shaggy Man," said he, taking another bite of the apple. "Just dropped in for a short call. Excuse my seeming haste."

Chapter Six

"Why, I s'pose you couldn't help the haste," said Betsy.

"No. I climbed an apple tree, outside; branch gave way and—here I am."

As he spoke the Shaggy Man finished his apple, gave the core to Hank—who ate it greedily—and then stood up to bow politely to Betsy and the Roses.

The Royal Gardener had been frightened nearly into fits by the crash of glass and the fall of the shaggy stranger into the bower of Roses, but now he peeped out from behind a bush and cried in his squeaky voice:

"You're breaking the Law! You're breaking the Law!"

Shaggy stared at him solemnly.

"Is the glass the Law in this country?" he asked.

"Breaking the glass is breaking the Law," squeaked the Gardener, angrily. "Also, to intrude in any part of the Rose Kingdom is breaking the Law."

"How do you know?" asked Shaggy.

"Why, it's printed in a book," said the Gardener, coming forward and taking a small book from his pocket. "Page thirteen. Here it is: 'If any stranger enters the Rose Kingdom he shall at once be condemned by the Ruler and put to death.' So you see, strangers," he continued triumphantly, "it's death for you all and your time has come!"

But just here Hank interposed. He had been stealthily backing toward the Royal Gardener, whom he disliked, and now the mule's heels shot out and struck the little man in the middle. He doubled up like the letter "U" and flew out of the door so swiftly—never touching the ground—that he was gone before Betsy had time to wink.

But the mule's attack frightened the girl.

"Come," she whispered, approaching the Shaggy Man and taking his hand; "let's go somewhere else. They'll surely kill us if we stay here!"

"Don't worry, my dear," replied Shaggy, patting the child's head. "I'm not afraid of anything, so long as I have the Love Magnet."

"The Love Magnet! Why, what is that?" asked Betsy.

"It's a charming little enchantment that wins the heart of everyone who looks upon it," was the reply. "The Love Magnet used to hang over the gateway to the Emerald City, in the Land of Oz; but when I started on this journey our beloved Ruler, Ozma of Oz, allowed me to take it with me."

"Oh!" cried Betsy, staring hard at him; "are you really from the wonderful Land of Oz?"

"Yes. Ever been there, my dear?"

"No; but I've heard about it. And do you know Princess Ozma?"

"Very well indeed."

"And—and Princess Dorothy?"

"Dorothy's an old chum of mine," declared Shaggy.

"Dear me!" exclaimed Betsy. "And why did you ever leave such a beautiful land as Oz?"

"On an errand," said Shaggy, looking sad and solemn. "I'm trying to find my dear little brother."

"Oh! Is he lost?" questioned Betsy, feeling very sorry for the poor man.

"Been lost these ten years," replied Shaggy, taking out a handkerchief and wiping a tear from his eye. "I didn't know it until lately, when I saw it recorded in the magic Record Book of the Sorceress Glinda, in the Land of Oz. So now I'm trying to find him."

"Where was he lost?" asked the girl sympathetically.

"Back in Colorado, where I used to live before I went to Oz. Brother was a miner, and dug gold out of a mine. One day he went into his mine and never came out. They searched for him, but he was not there. Disappeared entirely," Shaggy ended miserably.

"For goodness sake! What do you s'pose became of him?" she asked.

"There is only one explanation," replied Shaggy, taking another apple from his pocket and eating it to relieve his misery. "The Nome King probably got him."

"The Nome King! Who is he?"

"Why, he's sometimes called the Metal Monarch, and his name is Ruggedo. Lives in some underground cavern.

Claims to own all the metals hidden in the earth. Don't ask me why."

"Why?"

"'Cause I don't know. But this Ruggedo gets wild with anger if anyone digs gold out of the earth, and my private opinion is that he captured brother and carried him off to his underground kingdom. No—don't ask me why. I see you're dying to ask me why. But I don't know."

"But—dear me!—in that case you will never find your lost brother!" exclaimed the girl.

"Maybe not; but it's my duty to try," answered Shaggy. "I've wandered so far without finding him, but that only proves he is not where I've been looking. What I seek now is the hidden passage to the underground cavern of the terrible Metal Monarch."

"Well," said Betsy doubtfully, "it strikes me that if you ever manage to get there the Metal Monarch will make you, too, his prisoner."

"Nonsense!" answered Shaggy, carelessly. "You mustn't forget the Love Magnet."

"What about it?" she asked.

"When the fierce Metal Monarch sees the Love Magnet, he will love me dearly and do anything I ask."

"It must be wonderful," said Betsy, with awe.

"It is," the man assured her. "Shall I show it to you?"

"Oh, do!" she cried; so Shaggy searched in his shaggy pocket and drew out a small silver magnet, shaped like a horseshoe.

The moment Betsy saw it she began to like the Shaggy Man better than before. Hank also saw the Magnet and crept up to Shaggy to rub his head lovingly against the man's knee.

But they were interrupted by the Royal Gardener, who stuck his head into the greenhouse and shouted angrily:

"You are all condemned to death! Your only chance to escape is to leave here instantly."

This startled little Betsy, but the Shaggy Man merely waved the Magnet toward the Gardener, who, seeing it, rushed forward and threw himself at Shaggy's feet, murmuring in honeyed words:

"Oh, you lovely, lovely man! How fond I am of you! Every shag and bobtail that decorates you is dear to me—all I have is yours! But for goodness' sake get out of here before you die the death."

"I'm not going to die," declared Shaggy Man.

"You must. It's the Law," exclaimed the Gardener, beginning to weep real tears. "It breaks my heart to tell you this bad news, but the Law says that all strangers must be condemned by the Ruler to die the death."

"No Ruler has condemned us yet," said Betsy.

"Of course not," added Shaggy. "We haven't even seen the Ruler of the Rose Kingdom."

"Well, to tell the truth," said the Gardener, in a perplexed tone of voice, "we haven't any real Ruler, just now. You see, all our Rulers grow on bushes in the Royal Gardens, and the last one we had got mildewed and withered before his time. So we had to plant him, and at this time there is no one growing on the Royal Bushes who is ripe enough to pick."

"How do you know?" asked Betsy.

"Why, I'm the Royal Gardener. Plenty of royalties are growing, I admit; but just now they are all green. Until one ripens, I am supposed to rule the Rose Kingdom myself, and see that its Laws are obeyed. Therefore, much as I love you, Shaggy, I must put you to death."

"Wait a minute," pleaded Betsy. "I'd like to see those Royal Gardens before I die."

"So would I," added Shaggy Man. "Take us there, Gardener."

"Oh, I can't do that," objected the Gardener. But Shaggy again showed him the Love Magnet and after one glance at it the Gardener could no longer resist.

He led Shaggy, Betsy and Hank to the end of the great greenhouse and carefully unlocked a small door. Passing through this they came into the splendid Royal Garden of the Rose Kingdom.

Chapter Six

It was all surrounded by a tall hedge and within the enclosure grew several enormous rosebushes having thick green leaves of the texture of velvet. Upon these bushes grew the members of the Royal Family of the Rose Kingdom— men, women and children in all stages of maturity. They all seemed to have a light green hue, as if unripe or not fully developed, their flesh and clothing being alike green. They stood perfectly lifeless upon their branches, which swayed softly in the breeze, and their wide-open eyes stared straight ahead, unseeing and unintelligent.

While examining these curious growing people, Betsy passed behind a big central bush and at once uttered an exclamation of surprise and pleasure. For there, blooming in perfect color and shape, stood a Royal Princess, whose beauty was amazing.

"Why, she's ripe!" cried Betsy, pushing aside some of the broad leaves to observe her more clearly.

"Well, perhaps so," admitted the Gardener, who had come to the girl's side; "but she's a girl, and so we can't use her for a Ruler."

"No, indeed!" came a chorus of soft voices, and looking around Betsy discovered that all the Roses had followed them from the greenhouse and were now grouped before the entrance.

"You see," explained the Gardener, "the subjects of Rose

Kingdom don't want a girl Ruler. They want a King."

"A King! We want a King!" repeated the chorus of Roses.

"Isn't she Royal?" inquired Shaggy, admiring the lovely Princess.

"Of course, for she grows on a Royal Bush. This Princess is named Ozga, as she is a distant cousin of Ozma of Oz; and, were she but a man, we would joyfully hail her as our Ruler."

The Gardener then turned away to talk with his Roses and Betsy whispered to her companion: "Let's pick her, Shaggy."

"All right," said he. "If she's royal, she has the right to rule this Kingdom, and if we pick her she will surely protect us and prevent our being hurt, or driven away."

So Betsy and Shaggy each took an arm of the beautiful Rose Princess and a little twist of her feet set her free of the branch upon which she grew. Very gracefully she stepped down from the bush to the ground, where she bowed low to Betsy and Shaggy and said in a delightfully sweet voice: "I thank you."

But at the sound of these words the Gardener and the Roses turned and discovered that the Princess had been picked, and was now alive. Over every face flashed an expression of resentment and anger, and one of the Roses cried aloud:

"Audacious mortals! What have you done?"

"Picked a Princess for you, that's all," replied Betsy, cheerfully.

"But we won't have her! We want a King!" exclaimed a Jacque Rose, and another added with a voice of scorn: "No girl shall rule over us!"

The newly-picked Princess looked from one to another of her rebellious subjects in astonishment. A grieved look came over her exquisite features.

"Have I no welcome here, pretty subjects?" she asked gently. "Have I not come from my Royal Bush to be your Ruler?"

"You were picked by mortals, without our consent," replied the Moss Rose, coldly; "so we refuse to allow you to rule us."

"Turn her out, Gardener, with the others!" cried the Tea Rose.

"Just a second, please!" called Shaggy, taking the Love Magnet from his pocket. "I guess this will win their love, Princess. Here—take it in your hand and let the roses see it."

Princess Ozga took the Magnet and held it poised before the eyes of her subjects; but the Roses regarded it with calm disdain.

"Why, what's the matter?" demanded Shaggy in surprise. "The Magnet never failed to work before!"

"I know," said Betsy, nodding her head wisely. "These Roses have no hearts."

"That's it," agreed the Gardener. "They're pretty, and sweet, and alive; but still they are Roses. Their stems have thorns, but no hearts."

The Princess sighed and handed the Magnet to the Shaggy Man.

"What shall I do?" she asked sorrowfully.

"Turn her out, Gardener, with the others!" commanded the Roses. "We will have no Ruler until a man-rose—a King —is ripe enough to pick."

"Very well," said the Gardener meekly. "You must excuse me, my dear Shaggy, for opposing your wishes, but you and the others, including Ozga, must get out of Rose Kingdom immediately, if not before."

"Don't you love me, Gardy?" asked Shaggy, carelessly displaying the Magnet.

"I do. I dote on thee!" answered the Gardener earnestly; "but no true man will neglect his duty for the sake of love. My duty is to drive you out, so—out you go!"

With this he seized a garden fork and began jabbing it at the strangers, in order to force them to leave. Hank the mule was not afraid of the fork and when he got his heels near to the Gardener the man fell back to avoid a kick.

But now the Roses crowded around the outcasts and it

was soon discovered that beneath their draperies of green leaves were many sharp thorns which were more dangerous than Hank's heels. Neither Betsy nor Ozga nor Shaggy nor the mule cared to brave those thorns and when they pressed away from them they found themselves slowly driven through the garden door into the greenhouse. From there they were forced out at the entrance and so through the territory of the flower-strewn Rose Kingdom, which was not of very great extent.

The Rose Princess was sobbing bitterly; Betsy was indignant and angry; Hank uttered defiant "Hee-haws" and the Shaggy Man whistled softly to himself.

The boundary of the Rose Kingdom was a deep gulf, but there was a drawbridge in one place and this the Royal Gardener let down until the outcasts had passed over it. Then he drew it up again and returned with his Roses to the greenhouse, leaving the four queerly assorted comrades to wander into the bleak and unknown country that lay beyond.

"I don't mind, much," remarked Shaggy, as he led the way over the stony, barren ground. "I've got to search for my long-lost little brother, anyhow, so it won't matter where I go."

"Hank and I will help you find your brother," said Betsy in her most cheerful voice. "I'm so far away from home now that I don't s'pose I'll ever find my way back; and, to tell the truth, it's more fun traveling around and having adventures

than sticking at home. Don't you think so, Hank?"

"Hee-haw!" said Hank, and the Shaggy Man thanked them both.

"For my part," said Princess Ozga of Roseland, with a gentle sigh, "I must remain forever exiled from my Kingdom. So I, too, will be glad to help the Shaggy Man find his lost brother."

"That's very kind of you, ma'am," said Shaggy. "But unless I can find the underground cavern of Ruggedo,* the Metal Monarch, I shall never find poor brother."

"Doesn't anyone know where it is?" inquired Betsy.

"*Some* one must know, of course," was Shaggy's reply. "But we are not the ones. The only way to succeed is for us to keep going until we find a person who can direct us to Ruggedo's cavern."

"We may find it ourselves, without any help," suggested Betsy. "Who knows?"

"No one knows that, except the person who's writing this story," said Shaggy. "But we won't find anything—not even supper—unless we travel on. Here's a path. Let's take it and see where it leads to."

---

* This King was formerly named "Roquat," but after he drank of the "Waters of Oblivion" he forgot his own name and had to take another.

CHAPTER 7

Polychrome's Pitiful Plight

THE Rain King got too much water in his basin and spilled some over the brim. That made it rain in a certain part of the country—a real hard shower, for a time—and sent the Rainbow scampering to the place to show the gorgeous colors of his glorious bow as soon as the mist of rain had passed and the sky was clear.

The coming of the Rainbow is always a joyous event to earth folk, yet few have ever seen it close by. Usually the Rainbow is so far distant that you can observe its splendid hues but dimly, and that is why we seldom catch sight of the dancing Daughters of the Rainbow.

In the barren country where the rain had just fallen there

65

appeared to be no human beings at all; but the Rainbow appeared, just the same, and dancing gayly upon its arch were the Rainbow's Daughters, led by the fairylike Polychrome, who is so dainty and beautiful that no girl has ever quite equalled her in loveliness.

Polychrome was in a merry mood and danced down the arch of the bow to the ground, daring her sisters to follow her. Laughing and gleeful, they also touched the ground with their twinkling feet; but all the Daughters of the Rainbow knew that this was a dangerous pastime, so they quickly climbed upon their bow again.

All but Polychrome. Though the sweetest and merriest of them all, she was likewise the most reckless. Moreover, it was an unusual sensation to pat the cold, damp earth with her rosy toes. Before she realized it the bow had lifted and disappeared in the billowy blue sky, and here was Polychrome standing helpless upon a rock, her gauzy draperies floating about her like brilliant cobwebs and not a soul—fairy or mortal—to help her regain her lost bow!

"Dear me!" she exclaimed, a frown passing across her pretty face, "I'm caught again. This is the second time my carelessness has left me on earth while my sisters returned to our Sky Palaces. The first time I enjoyed some pleasant adventures, but this is a lonely, forsaken country and I shall be very unhappy until my Rainbow comes again and I can climb aboard. Let me think what is best to be done."

She crouched low upon the flat rock, drew her draperies about her and bowed her head.

It was in this position that Betsy Bobbin spied Polychrome as she came along the stony path, followed by Hank, the Princess and Shaggy. At once the girl ran up to the radiant Daughter of the Rainbow and exclaimed:

"Oh, what a lovely, lovely creature!"

Polychrome raised her golden head. There were tears in her blue eyes.

"I'm the most miserable girl in the whole world!" she sobbed.

The others gathered around her.

"Tell us your troubles, pretty one," urged the Princess.

"I—I've lost my bow!" wailed Polychrome.

"Take me, my dear," said Shaggy Man in a sympathetic tone, thinking she meant "beau" instead of "bow."

"I don't want you!" cried Polychrome, stamping her foot imperiously; "I want my *Rain*bow."

"Oh; that's different," said Shaggy. "But try to forget it. When I was young I used to cry for the Rainbow myself, but I couldn't have it. Looks as if *you* couldn't have it, either; so please don't cry."

Polychrome looked at him reproachfully.

"I don't like you," she said.

"No?" replied Shaggy, drawing the Love Magnet from his pocket; "not a little bit?—just a wee speck of a like?"

"Yes, yes!" said Polychrome, clasping her hands in ecstasy as she gazed at the enchanted talisman; "I love you, Shaggy Man!"

"Of course you do," said he calmly; "but I don't take any credit for it. It's the Love Magnet's powerful charm. But you seem quite alone and friendless, little Rainbow. Don't you want to join our party until you find your father and sisters again?"

"Where are you going?" she asked.

"We don't just know that," said Betsy, taking her hand; "but we're trying to find Shaggy's long-lost brother, who has been captured by the terrible Metal Monarch. Won't you come with us, and help us?"

Polychrome looked from one to another of the queer party of travelers and a bewitching smile suddenly lighted her face.

"A donkey, a mortal maid, a Rose Princess and a Shaggy Man!" she exclaimed. "Surely you need help, if you intend to face Ruggedo."

"Do you know him, then?" inquired Betsy.

"No, indeed. Ruggedo's caverns are beneath the earth's surface, where no Rainbow can ever penetrate. But I've heard of the Metal Monarch. He is also called the Nome King, you know, and he has made trouble for a good many people—mortals and fairies—in his time," said Polychrome.

"Do you fear him, then?" asked the Princess, anxiously.

"No one can harm a Daughter of the Rainbow," said Polychrome proudly. "I'm a sky fairy."

"Then," said Betsy, quickly, "you will be able to tell us the way to Ruggedo's cavern."

"No," returned Polychrome, shaking her head, "that is one thing I cannot do. But I will gladly go with you and help you search for the place."

This promise delighted all the wanderers and after the Shaggy Man had found the path again they began moving along it in a more happy mood. The Rainbow's Daughter danced lightly over the rocky trail, no longer sad, but with her beautiful features wreathed in smiles. Shaggy came next, walking steadily and now and then supporting the Rose Princess, who followed him. Betsy and Hank brought up the rear, and if she tired with walking the girl got upon Hank's back and let the stout little donkey carry her for awhile.

At nightfall they came to some trees that grew beside a tiny brook and here they made camp and rested until morning. Then away they tramped, finding berries and fruits here and there which satisfied the hunger of Betsy, Shaggy and Hank, so that they were well content with their lot.

It surprised Betsy to see the Rose Princess partake of their food, for she considered her a fairy; but when she mentioned this to Polychrome, the Rainbow's Daughter explained that when Ozga was driven out of her Rose Kingdom she ceased to be a fairy and would never again be more than a mere mortal. Polychrome, however, was a fairy wherever she happened to be, and if she sipped a few dewdrops by moonlight for refreshment no one ever saw her do it.

As they continued their wandering journey, direction meant very little to them, for they were hopelessly lost in this strange country. Shaggy said it would be best to go toward the mountains, as the natural entrance to Ruggedo's underground cavern was likely to be hidden in some rocky, deserted place; but mountains seemed all around them except in the one direction that they had come from, which led to the Rose Kingdom and the sea. Therefore it mattered little which way they traveled.

By and by they espied a faint trail that looked like a path and after following this for some time they reached a crossroads. Here were many paths, leading in various directions, and there was a signpost so old that there were now no words upon the sign. At one side was an old well, with a chain windlass for drawing water, yet there was no house or other building anywhere in sight.

While the party halted, puzzled which way to proceed, the mule approached the well and tried to look into it.

Chapter Seven

"He's thirsty," said Betsy.

"It's a dry well," remarked Shaggy. "Probably there has been no water in it for many years. But, come; let us decide which way to travel."

No one seemed able to decide that. They sat down in a group and tried to consider which road might be the best to take. Hank, however, could not keep away from the well and finally he reared up on his hind legs, got his head over the edge and uttered a loud "Hee-haw!" Betsy watched her animal friend curiously.

"I wonder if he sees anything down there?" she said.

At this, Shaggy rose and went over to the well to investigate, and Betsy went with him. The Princess and Polychrome, who had become fast friends, linked arms and sauntered down one of the roads, to find an easy path.

"Really," said Shaggy, "there does seem to be something at the bottom of this old well."

"Can't we pull it up, and see what it is?" asked the girl.

There was no bucket at the end of the windlass chain, but there was a big hook that at one time was used to hold a bucket. Shaggy let down this hook, dragged it around on the bottom and then pulled it up. An old hoopskirt came with it, and Betsy laughed and threw it away. The thing frightened Hank, who had never seen a hoopskirt before, and he kept a good distance away from it.

Several other objects the Shaggy Man captured with the hook and drew up, but none of these was important.

"This well seems to have been the dump for all the old rubbish in the country," he said, letting down the hook once more. "I guess I've captured everything now. No—the hook has caught again. Help me, Betsy! Whatever this thing is, it's heavy."

She ran up and helped him turn the windlass and after much effort a confused mass of copper came in sight.

"Good gracious!" exclaimed Shaggy. "Here is a surprise, indeed!"

"What is it?" inquired Betsy, clinging to the windlass and panting for breath.

For answer the Shaggy Man grasped the bundle of copper and dumped it upon the ground, free of the well. Then he turned it over with his foot, spread it out, and to Betsy's astonishment the thing proved to be a copper man.

"Just as I thought," said Shaggy, looking hard at the object. "But unless there are two copper men in the world this is the most astonishing thing I ever came across."

At this moment the Rainbow's Daughter and the Rose Princess approached them, and Polychrome said:

"What have you found, Shaggy One?"

"Either an old friend, or a stranger," he replied.

"Oh, here's a sign on his back!" cried Betsy, who had

knelt down to examine the man. "Dear me; how funny! Listen to this."

Then she read the following words, engraved upon the copper plates of the man's body:

SMITH & TINKER'S

Patent Double-Action, Extra-Responsive,
Thought-Creating, Perfect-Talking
MECHANICAL MAN
Fitted with our Special Clockwork Attachment.
Thinks, Speaks, Acts, and Does Everything but Live.

"Isn't he wonderful!" exclaimed the Princess.

"Yes; but here's more," said Betsy, reading from another engraved plate:

DIRECTIONS FOR USING:

For THINKING:—Wind the Clockwork Man under his left arm, (marked No. 1).

For SPEAKING:—Wind the Clockwork Man under his right arm, (marked No. 2).

For WALKING and ACTION:—Wind Clockwork Man in the middle of his back, (marked No. 3).

N. B.—This Mechanism is guaranteed to work perfectly for a thousand years.

"If he's guaranteed for a thousand years," said Polychrome, "he ought to work yet."

"Of course," replied Shaggy. "Let's wind him up."

In order to do this they were obliged to set the copper man upon his feet, in an upright position, and this was no easy task. He was inclined to topple over, and had to be propped again and again. The girls assisted Shaggy, and at last Tik-Tok seemed to be balanced and stood alone upon his broad feet.

"Yes," said Shaggy, looking at the copper man carefully, "this must be, indeed, my old friend Tik-Tok, whom I left ticking merrily in the Land of Oz. But how he came to this lonely place, and got into that old well, is surely a mystery."

"If we wind him, perhaps he will tell us," suggested Betsy. "Here's the key, hanging to a hook on his back. What part of him shall I wind up first?"

"His thoughts, of course," said Polychrome, "for it requires thought to speak or move intelligently."

So Betsy wound him under his left arm, and at once little flashes of light began to show in the top of his head, which was proof that he had begun to think.

"Now, then," said Shaggy, "wind up his phonograph."

"What's that?" she asked.

"Why, his talking-machine. His thoughts may be interesting, but they don't tell us anything."

Chapter Seven

So Betsy wound the copper man under his right arm, and then from the interior of his copper body came in jerky tones the words: "Ma-ny thanks!"

"Hurrah!" cried Shaggy, joyfully, and he slapped Tik-Tok upon the back in such a hearty manner that the copper man lost his balance and tumbled to the ground in a heap. But the clockwork that enabled him to speak had been wound up and he kept saying: "Pick-me-up! Pick-me-up! Pick-me-up!" until they had again raised him and balanced him upon his feet, when he added politely: "Ma-ny thanks!"

"He won't be self-supporting until we wind up his action," remarked Shaggy; so Betsy wound it, as tight as she could—for the key turned rather hard—and then Tik-Tok lifted his feet, marched around in a circle and ended by stopping before the group and making them all a low bow.

"How in the world did you happen to be in that well, when I left you safe in Oz?" inquired Shaggy.

"It is a long sto-ry," replied Tik-Tok, "but I'll tell it in a few words. Af-ter you had gone in search of your broth-er, Oz-ma saw you wan-der-ing in strange lands when-ev-er she looked in her mag-ic pic-ture, and she also saw your broth-er in the Nome King's cav-ern; so she sent me to tell you where to find your broth-er and told me to help you if I could. The Sor-cer-ess, Glin-da the Good, trans-port-ed me to this place in the wink of an eye; but here I met the Nome King him-

75

self—old Rug-ge-do, who is called in these parts the Met-al Mon-arch. Rug-ge-do knew what I had come for, and he was so an-gry that he threw me down the well. Af-ter my works ran down I was help-less un-til you came a-long and pulled me out a-gain. Ma-ny thanks."

"This is, indeed, good news," said Shaggy. "I suspected that my brother was the prisoner of Ruggedo; but now I know it. Tell us, Tik-Tok, how shall we get to the Nome King's underground cavern?"

"The best way is to walk," said Tik-Tok. "We might crawl, or jump, or roll o-ver and o-ver un-til we get there; but the best way is to walk."

"I know; but which road shall we take?"

"My ma-chin-er-y is-n't made to tell that," replied Tik-Tok.

"There is more than one entrance to the underground cavern," said Polychrome; "but old Ruggedo has cleverly con-cealed every opening, so that earth dwellers can not intrude in his domain. If we find our way underground at all, it will be by chance."

"Then," said Betsy, "let us select any road, haphazard, and see where it leads us."

"That seems sensible," declared the Princess. "It may require a lot of time for us to find Ruggedo, but we have more time than anything else."

"If you keep me wound up," said Tik-Tok, "I will last a thou-sand years."

"Then the only question to decide is which way to go," added Shaggy, looking first at one road and then at another.

But while they stood hesitating, a peculiar sound reached their ears—a sound like the tramping of many feet.

"What's coming?" cried Betsy; and then she ran to the left-hand road and glanced along the path. "Why, it's an army!" she exclaimed. "What shall we do, hide or run?"

"Stand still," commanded Shaggy. "I'm not afraid of an army. If they prove to be friendly, they can help us; if they are enemies, I'll show them the Love Magnet."

CHAPTER 8

Tik-Tok Tackles a Tough Task

WHILE Shaggy and his companions stood huddled in a group at one side, the Army of Oogaboo was approaching along the pathway, the tramp of their feet being now and then accompanied by a dismal groan as one of the officers stepped on a sharp stone or knocked his funnybone against his neighbor's sword-handle.

Then out from among the trees marched Private Files, bearing the banner of Oogaboo, which fluttered from a long pole. This pole he stuck in the ground just in front of the well and then he cried in a loud voice:

"I hereby conquer this territory in the name of Queen Ann Soforth of Oogaboo, and all the inhabitants of the land I proclaim her slaves!"

78

Chapter Eight

Some of the officers now stuck their heads out of the bushes and asked:

"Is the coast clear, Private Files?"

"There is no coast here," was the reply, "but all's well."

"I hope there's water in it," said General Cone, mustering courage to advance to the well; but just then he caught a glimpse of Tik-Tok and Shaggy and at once fell upon his knees, trembling and frightened, and cried out:

"Mercy, kind enemies! Mercy! Spare us, and we will be your slaves forever!"

The other officers, who had now advanced into the clearing, likewise fell upon their knees and begged for mercy.

Files turned around and, seeing the strangers for the first time, examined them with much curiosity. Then, discovering that three of the party were girls, he lifted his cap and made a polite bow.

"What's all this?" demanded a harsh voice, as Queen Ann reached the place and beheld her kneeling army.

"Permit us to introduce ourselves," replied Shaggy, stepping forward. "This is Tik-Tok, the Clockwork Man—who works better than some meat people. And here is Princess Ozga of Roseland, just now unfortunately exiled from her Kingdom of Roses. I next present Polychrome, a sky fairy, who lost her Bow by an accident and can't find her way home. The small girl here is Betsy Bobbin, from some unknown earthly paradise called Oklahoma, and with her you see Mr. Hank, a mule with a long tail and a short temper."

"Puh!" said Ann, scornfully; "a pretty lot of vagabonds you are, indeed; all lost or strayed, I suppose, and not worth a Queen's plundering. I'm sorry I've conquered you."

"But you haven't conquered us yet," called Betsy indignantly.

"No," agreed Files, "that is a fact. But if my officers will kindly command me to conquer you, I will do so at once, after which we can stop arguing and converse more at our ease."

The officers had by this time risen from their knees and brushed the dust from their trousers. To them the enemy did not look very fierce, so the Generals and Colonels and Majors and Captains gained courage to face them and began strutting in their most haughty manner.

"You must understand," said Ann, "that I am the Queen of Oogaboo, and this is my invincible Army. We are busy conquering the world, and since you seem to be a part of the world, and are obstructing our journey, it is necessary for us to conquer you—unworthy though you may be of such high honor."

"That's all right," replied Shaggy. "Conquer us as often as you like. We don't mind."

"But we won't be anybody's slaves," added Betsy, positively.

"We'll see about that," retorted the Queen, angrily. "Advance, Private Files, and bind the enemy hand and foot!"

But Private Files looked at pretty Betsy and fascinating Polychrome and the beautiful Rose Princess and shook his head.

"It would be impolite, and I won't do it," he asserted.

"You must!" cried Ann. "It is your duty to obey orders."

"I haven't received any orders from my officers," objected the Private.

But the Generals now shouted: "Forward, and bind the prisoners!" and the Colonels and Majors and Captains repeated the command, yelling it as loud as they could.

All this noise annoyed Hank, who had been eyeing the Army of Oogaboo with strong disfavor. The mule now dashed forward and began backing upon the officers and kicking fierce and dangerous heels at them. The attack was so sudden that the officers scattered like dust in a whirlwind, dropping their swords as they ran and trying to seek refuge behind the trees and bushes.

Betsy laughed joyously at the comical rout of the "noble army," and Polychrome danced with glee. But Ann was furious at this ignoble defeat of her gallant forces by one small mule.

"Private Files, I command you to do your duty!" she

cried again, and then she herself ducked to escape the mule's heels—for Hank made no distinction in favor of a lady who was an open enemy. Betsy grabbed her champion by the forelock, however, and so held him fast, and when the officers saw that the mule was restrained from further attacks they crept fearfully back and picked up their discarded swords.

"Private Files, seize and bind these prisoners!" screamed the Queen.

"No," said Files, throwing down his gun and removing the knapsack which was strapped to his back, "I resign my position as the Army of Oogaboo. I enlisted to fight the enemy and become a hero, but if you want some one to bind harmless girls you will have to hire another Private."

Then he walked over to the others and shook hands with Shaggy and Tik-Tok.

"Treason!" shrieked Ann, and all the officers echoed her cry.

"Nonsense," said Files. "I've the right to resign if I want to."

"Indeed you haven't!" retorted the Queen. "If you resign it will break up my Army, and then I cannot conquer the world." She now turned to the officers and said: "I must ask you to do me a favor. I know it is undignified in officers to fight, but unless you immediately capture Private Files and force him to obey my orders there will be no plunder for any of us. Also it is likely you will all suffer the pangs of hunger, and when we meet a powerful foe you are liable to be captured and made slaves."

The prospect of this awful fate so frightened the officers that they drew their swords and rushed upon Files, who stood beside Shaggy, in a truly ferocious manner. The next instant, however, they halted and again fell upon their knees; for there, before them, was the glistening Love Magnet, held in the hand of the smiling Shaggy Man, and the sight of this magic talisman at once won the heart of every Oogabooite. Even Ann saw the Love Magnet, and forgetting all enmity and anger threw herself upon Shaggy and embraced him lovingly.

Quite disconcerted by this unexpected effect of the Magnet, Shaggy disengaged himself from the Queen's encircling arms and quickly hid the talisman in his pocket. The adventurers from Oogaboo were now his firm friends, and there was no more talk about conquering and binding any of his party.

"If you insist on conquering anyone," said Shaggy, "you may march with me to the underground Kingdom of Ruggedo. To conquer the world, as you have set out to do, you must conquer everyone under its surface as well as those upon its surface, and no one in all the world needs conquering so much as Ruggedo."

"Who is he?" asked Ann.

"The Metal Monarch, King of the Nomes."

"Is he rich?" inquired Major Stockings in an anxious voice.

"Of course," answered Shaggy. "He owns all the metal that lies underground—gold, silver, copper, brass and tin. He has an idea he also owns all the metals above ground, for he says all metal was once a part of his kingdom. So, by conquering the Metal Monarch, you will win all the riches in the world."

"Ah!" exclaimed General Apple, heaving a deep sigh, "that would be plunder worth our while. Let's conquer him, Your Majesty."

The Queen looked reproachfully at Files, who was sitting next to the lovely Princess and whispering in her ear.

"Alas," said Ann, "I have no longer an Army. I have plenty of brave officers, indeed, but no private soldier for them to command. Therefore I cannot conquer Ruggedo and win all his wealth."

"Why don't you make one of your officers the Private?" asked Shaggy; but at once every officer began to protest and the Queen of Oogaboo shook her head as she replied:

"That is impossible. A private soldier must be a terrible fighter, and my officers are unable to fight. They are exceptionally brave in commanding others to fight, but could not themselves meet the enemy and conquer."

"Very true, Your Majesty," said Colonel Plum, eagerly. "There are many kinds of bravery and one cannot be expected to possess them all. I myself am brave as a lion in all ways until it comes to fighting, but then my nature revolts. Fighting is unkind and liable to be injurious to others; so, being a gentleman, I never fight."

"Nor I!" shouted each of the other officers.

"You see," said Ann, "how helpless I am. Had not Private Files proved himself a traitor and a deserter, I would gladly have conquered this Ruggedo; but an Army without a private soldier is like a bee without a stinger."

"I am not a traitor, Your Majesty," protested Files. "I resigned in a proper manner, not liking the job. But there are plenty of people to take my place. Why not make Shaggy Man the private soldier?"

"He might be killed," said Ann, looking tenderly at Shaggy, "for he is mortal, and able to die. If anything happened to him, it would break my heart."

"It would hurt me worse than that," declared Shaggy. "You must admit, Your Majesty, that I am commander of this expedition, for it is my brother we are seeking, rather than plunder. But I and my companions would like the assistance of your Army, and if you help us to conquer Ruggedo and to rescue my brother from captivity we will allow you to keep all the gold and jewels and other plunder you may find."

Tik-Tok of Oz

This prospect was so tempting that the officers began whispering together and presently Colonel Cheese said: "Your Majesty, by combining our brains we have just evolved a most brilliant idea. We will make the Clockwork Man the private soldier!"

"Who? Me?" asked Tik-Tok. "Not for a sin-gle sec-ond! I can-not fight, and you must not for-get that it was Rug-ge-do who threw me in the well."

"At that time you had no gun," said Polychrome. "But if you join the Army of Oogaboo you will carry the gun that Mr. Files used."

"A sol-dier must be a-ble to run as well as to fight," protested Tik-Tok, "and if my works run down, as they of-ten do, I could nei-ther run nor fight."

"I'll keep you wound up, Tik-Tok," promised Betsy.

"Why, it isn't a bad idea," said Shaggy. "Tik-Tok will make an ideal soldier, for nothing can injure him except a sledge hammer. And, since a private soldier seems to be necessary to this Army, Tik-Tok is the only one of our party fitted to undertake the job."

"What must I do?" asked Tik-Tok.

"Obey orders," replied Ann. "When the officers command you to do anything, you must do it; that is all."

"And that's enough, too," said Files.

"Do I get a salary?" inquired Tik-Tok.

Chapter Eight

"You get your share of the plunder," answered the Queen.

"Yes," remarked Files, "one-half of the plunder goes to Queen Ann, the other half is divided among the officers, and the Private gets the rest."

"That will be sat-is-fac-tor-y," said Tik-Tok, picking up the gun and examining it wonderingly, for he had never before seen such a weapon.

Then Ann strapped the knapsack to Tik-Tok's copper back and said: "Now we are ready to march to Ruggedo's Kingdom and conquer it. Officers, give the command to march."

"Fall—in!" yelled the Generals, drawing their swords.

"Fall—in!" cried the Colonels, drawing their swords.

"Fall—in!" shouted the Majors, drawing their swords.

"Fall—in!" bawled the Captains, drawing their swords.

Tik-Tok looked at them and then around him in surprise.

"Fall in what? The well?" he asked.

"No," said Queen Ann, "you must fall in marching order."

"Can-not I march with-out fall-ing in-to it?" asked the Clockwork Man.

"Shoulder your gun and stand ready to march," advised Files; so Tik-Tok held the gun straight and stood still.

"What next?" he asked.

The Queen turned to Shaggy.

"Which road leads to the Metal Monarch's cavern?"

89

"We don't know, Your Majesty," was the reply.

"But this is absurd!" said Ann with a frown. "If we can't get to Ruggedo, it is certain that we can't conquer him."

"You are right," admitted Shaggy; "but I did not say we could not get to him. We have only to discover the way, and that was the matter we were considering when you and your magnificent Army arrived here."

"Well, then, get busy and discover it," snapped the Queen.

That was no easy task. They all stood looking from one road to another in perplexity. The paths radiated from the little clearing like the rays of the midday sun, and each path seemed like all the others.

Files and the Rose Princess, who had by this time become good friends, advanced a little way along one of the roads and found that it was bordered by pretty wild flowers.

"Why don't you ask the flowers to tell you the way?" he said to his companion.

"The flowers?" returned the Princess, surprised at the question.

"Of course," said Files. "The field-flowers must be second-cousins to a Rose Princess, and I believe if you ask them they will tell you."

She looked more closely at the flowers. There were hundreds of white daisies, golden buttercups, bluebells and

daffodils growing by the roadside, and each flower-head was firmly set upon its slender but stout stem. There were even a few wild roses scattered here and there and perhaps it was the sight of these that gave the Princess courage to ask the important question.

She dropped to her knees, facing the flowers, and extended both her arms pleadingly toward them.

"Tell me, pretty cousins," she said in her sweet, gentle voice, "which way will lead us to the Kingdom of Ruggedo, the Nome King?"

At once all the stems bent gracefully to the right and the flower heads nodded once—twice—thrice in that direction.

"That's it!" cried Files joyfully. "Now we know the way."

Ozga rose to her feet and looked wonderingly at the field-flowers, which had now resumed their upright position.

"Was it the wind, do you think?" she asked in a low whisper.

"No, indeed," replied Files. "There is not a breath of wind stirring. But these lovely blossoms are indeed your cousins and answered your question at once, as I knew they would."

CHAPTER 9

Ruggedo's Rage is Rash and Reckless

THE way taken by the adventurers led up hill and down dale and wound here and there in a fashion that seemed aimless. But always it drew nearer to a range of low mountains and Files said more than once that he was certain the entrance to Ruggedo's cavern would be found among these rugged hills.

In this he was quite correct. Far underneath the nearest mountain was a gorgeous chamber hollowed from the solid rock, the walls and roof of which glittered with thousands of magnificent jewels. Here, on a throne of virgin gold, sat the famous Nome King, dressed in splendid robes and wearing a superb crown cut from a single blood-red ruby.

Chapter Nine

Ruggedo, the Monarch of all the Metals and Precious Stones of the Underground World, was a round little man with a flowing white beard, a red face, bright eyes and a scowl that covered all his forehead. One would think, to look at him, that he ought to be jolly; one might think, considering his enormous wealth, that he ought to be happy; but this was not the case. The Metal Monarch was surly and cross because mortals had dug so much treasure out of the earth and kept it above ground, where all the power of Ruggedo and his nomes was unable to recover it. He hated not only the mortals but also the fairies who live upon the earth or above it, and instead of being content with the riches he still possessed he was unhappy because he did not own all the gold and jewels in the world.

Ruggedo had been nodding, half asleep, in his chair when suddenly he sat upright, uttered a roar of rage and began pounding upon a huge gong that stood beside him.

The sound filled the vast cavern and penetrated to many caverns beyond, where countless thousands of nomes were working at their unending tasks, hammering out gold and silver and other metals, or melting ores in great furnaces, or polishing glittering gems. The nomes trembled at the sound of the King's gong and whispered fearfully to one another that something unpleasant was sure to happen; but none dared pause in his task.

Tik-Tok of Oz

The heavy curtains of cloth-of-gold were pushed aside and Kaliko, the King's High Chamberlain, entered the royal presence.

"What's up, Your Majesty?" he asked, with a wide yawn, for he had just wakened.

"Up?" roared Ruggedo, stamping his foot viciously. "Those foolish mortals are up, that's what! And they want to come down."

"Down here?" inquired Kaliko.

"Yes!"

"How do you know?" continued the Chamberlain, yawning again.

"I feel it in my bones," said Ruggedo. "I can always feel it when those hateful earth-crawlers draw near to my Kingdom. I am positive, Kaliko, that mortals are this very minute on their way here to annoy me—and I hate mortals more than I do catnip tea!"

"Well, what's to be done?" demanded the nome.

"Look through your spyglass, and see where the invaders are," commanded the King.

So Kaliko went to a tube in the wall of rock and put his eye to it. The tube ran from the cavern up to the side of the mountain and turned several curves and corners, but as it was a magic spyglass Kaliko was able to see through it just as easily as if it had been straight.

94

Chapter Nine

"Ho—hum," said he. "I see 'em, Your Majesty."

"What do they look like?" inquired the Monarch.

"That's a hard question to answer, for a queerer assortment of creatures I never yet beheld," replied the nome. "However, such a collection of curiosities may prove dangerous. There's a copper man, worked by machinery—"

"Bah! that's only Tik-Tok," said Ruggedo. "I'm not afraid of him. Why, only the other day I met the fellow and threw him down a well."

"Then some one must have pulled him out again," said Kaliko. "And there's a little girl—"

"Dorothy?" asked Ruggedo, jumping up in fear.

"No; some other girl. In fact, there are several girls, of various sizes; but Dorothy is not with them, nor is Ozma."

"That's good!" exclaimed the King, sighing in relief.

Kaliko still had his eye to the spyglass.

"I see," said he, "an army of men from Oogaboo. They are all officers and carry swords. And there is a Shaggy Man —who seems very harmless—and a little donkey with big ears."

"Pooh!" cried Ruggedo, snapping his fingers in scorn. "I've no fear of such a mob as that. A dozen of my nomes can destroy them all in a jiffy."

"I'm not so sure of that," said Kaliko. "The people of Oogaboo are hard to destroy, and I believe the Rose Princess is a fairy. As for Polychrome, you know very well that the Rainbow's Daughter cannot be injured by a nome."

"Polychrome! Is she among them?" asked the King.

"Yes; I have just recognized her."

"Then these people are coming here on no peaceful errand," declared Ruggedo, scowling fiercely. "In fact, no one ever comes here on a peaceful errand. I hate everybody, and everybody hates me!"

"Very true," said Kaliko.

"I must in some way prevent these people from reaching my dominions. Where are they now?"

"Just now they are crossing the Rubber Country, Your Majesty."

"Good! Are your magnetic rubber wires in working order?"

"I think so," replied Kaliko. "Is it your Royal Will that we have some fun with these invaders?"

"It is," answered Ruggedo. "I want to teach them a lesson they will never forget."

Now, Shaggy had no idea that he was in a Rubber Country, nor had any of his companions. They noticed that everything around them was of a dull gray color and that the path upon which they walked was soft and springy, yet they had no suspicion that the rocks and trees were rubber and even the path they trod was made of rubber.

Chapter Nine

Presently they came to a brook where sparkling water dashed through a deep channel and rushed away between high rocks far down the mountain-side. Across the brook were stepping-stones, so placed that travelers might easily leap from one to another and in that manner cross the water to the farther bank.

Tik-Tok was marching ahead, followed by his officers and Queen Ann. After them came Betsy Bobbin and Hank, Polychrome and Shaggy, and last of all the Rose Princess with Files. The Clockwork Man saw the stream and the stepping-stones and, without making a pause, placed his foot upon the first stone.

The result was astonishing. First he sank down in the soft rubber, which then rebounded and sent Tik-Tok soaring high in the air, where he turned a succession of flip-flops and alighted upon a rubber rock far in the rear of the party.

General Apple did not see Tik-Tok bound, so quickly had he disappeared; therefore he also stepped upon the stone (which you will guess was connected with Kaliko's magnetic rubber wire) and instantly shot upward like an arrow. General Cone came next and met with a like fate, but the others now noticed that something was wrong and with one accord they halted the column and looked back along the path.

There was Tik-Tok, still bounding from one rubber rock to another, each time rising a less distance from the ground.

97

And there was General Apple, bounding away in another direction, his three-cornered hat jammed over his eyes and his long sword thumping him upon the arms and head as it swung this way and that. And there, also, appeared General Cone, who had struck a rubber rock headforemost and was so crumpled up that his round body looked more like a bouncing-ball than the form of a man.

Betsy laughed merrily at the strange sight and Polychrome echoed her laughter. But Ozga was grave and wondering, while Queen Ann became angry at seeing the chief officers of the Army of Oogaboo bounding around in so undignified a manner. She shouted to them to stop, but they were unable to obey, even though they would have been glad to do so. Finally, however, they all ceased bounding and managed to get upon their feet and rejoin the Army.

"Why did you do that?" demanded Ann, who seemed greatly provoked.

"Don't ask them why," said Shaggy earnestly. "I knew you would ask them why, but you ought not to do it. The reason is plain. Those stones are rubber; therefore they are not stones. Those rocks around us are rubber, and therefore they are not rocks. Even this path is not a path; it's rubber. Unless we are very careful, your Majesty, we are all likely to get the bounce, just as your poor officers and Tik-Tok did."

"Then let's be careful," remarked Files, who was full of

wisdom; but Polychrome wanted to test the quality of the rubber, so she began dancing. Every step sent her higher and higher into the air, so that she resembled a big butterfly fluttering lightly. Presently she made a great bound and bounded way across the stream, landing lightly and steadily on the other side.

"There is no rubber over here," she called to them. "Suppose you all try to bound over the stream, without touching the stepping-stones."

Ann and her officers were reluctant to undertake such a risky adventure, but Betsy at once grasped the value of the suggestion and began jumping up and down until she found herself bounding almost as high as Polychrome had done. Then she suddenly leaned forward and the next bound took her easily across the brook, where she alighted by the side of the Rainbow's Daughter.

"Come on, Hank!" called the girl, and the donkey tried to obey. He managed to bound pretty high but when he tried to bound across the stream he misjudged the distance and fell with a splash into the middle of the water.

"Hee-haw!" he wailed, struggling toward the far bank. Betsy rushed forward to help him out, but when the mule stood safely beside her she was amazed to find he was not wet at all.

"It's dry water," said Polychrome, dipping her hand into

the stream and showing how the water fell from it and left it perfectly dry.

"In that case," returned Betsy, "they can all walk through the water."

She called to Ozga and Shaggy to wade across, assuring them the water was shallow and would not wet them. At once they followed her advice, avoiding the rubber stepping-stones, and made the crossing with ease. This encouraged the entire party to wade through the dry water, and in a few minutes all had assembled on the bank and renewed their journey along the path that led to the Nome King's dominions.

When Kaliko again looked through his magic spyglass he exclaimed:

"Bad luck, Your Majesty! All the invaders have passed the Rubber Country and now are fast approaching the entrance to your caverns."

Ruggedo raved and stormed at the news and his anger was so great that several times, as he strode up and down his jeweled cavern, he paused to kick Kaliko upon his shins, which were so sensitive that the poor nome howled with pain. Finally the King said:

"There's no help for it; we must drop these audacious invaders down the Hollow Tube."

Kaliko gave a jump, at this, and looked at his master wonderingly.

"If you do that, Your Majesty," he said, "you will make Tititi-Hoochoo very angry."

"Never mind that," retorted Ruggedo. "Tititi-Hoochoo lives on the other side of the world, so what do I care for his anger?"

Kaliko shuddered and uttered a little groan.

"Remember his terrible powers," he pleaded, "and remember that he warned you, the last time you slid people through the Hollow Tube, that if you did it again he would take vengeance upon you."

The Metal Monarch walked up and down in silence, thinking deeply.

"Of two dangers," said he, "it is wise to choose the least. What do you suppose these invaders want?"

"Let the Long-Eared Hearer listen to them," suggested Kaliko.

"Call him here at once!" commanded Ruggedo eagerly.

So in a few minutes there entered the cavern a nome with enormous ears, who bowed low before the King.

"Strangers are approaching," said Ruggedo, "and I wish to know their errand. Listen carefully to their talk and tell me why they are coming here, and what for."

The nome bowed again and spread out his great ears, swaying them gently up and down and back and forth. For half an hour he stood silent, in an attitude of listening, while both

the King and Kaliko grew impatient at the delay. At last the Long-Eared Hearer spoke:

"Shaggy Man is coming here to rescue his brother from captivity," said he.

"Ha, the Ugly One!" exclaimed Ruggedo. "Well, Shaggy Man may have his ugly brother, for all I care. He's too lazy to work and is always getting in my way. Where is the Ugly One now, Kaliko?"

"The last time Your Majesty stumbled over the prisoner you commanded me to send him to the Metal Forest. which I did. I suppose he is still there."

"Very good. The invaders will have a hard time finding the Metal Forest," said the King, with a grin of malicious delight, "for half the time I can't find it myself. Yet I created the forest and made every tree, out of gold and silver, so as to keep the precious metals in a safe place and out of the reach of mortals. But tell me, Hearer, do the strangers want anything else?"

"Yes, indeed they do!" returned the nome. "The Army of Oogaboo is determined to capture all the rich metals and rare jewels in your kingdom, and the officers and their Queen have arranged to divide the spoils and carry them away."

When he heard this Ruggedo uttered a bellow of rage and began dancing up and down, rolling his eyes, clicking his teeth together and swinging his arms furiously. Then, in an ecstasy of anger he seized the long ears of the Hearer and pulled and twisted them cruelly; but Kaliko grabbed up the King's sceptre and rapped him over the knuckles with it, so that Ruggedo let go the ears and began to chase his Royal Chamberlain around the throne.

The Hearer took advantage of this opportunity to slip away from the cavern and escape, and after the King had tired himself out chasing Kaliko he threw himself into his throne and panted for breath, while he glared wickedly at his defiant subject.

"You'd better save your strength to fight the enemy," suggested Kaliko. "There will be a terrible battle when the Army of Oogaboo gets here."

"The Army won't get here," said the King, still coughing and panting. "I'll drop 'em down the Hollow Tube—every man Jack and every girl Jill of 'em!"

"And defy Tititi-Hoochoo?" asked Kaliko.

"Yes. Go at once to my Chief Magician and order him to turn the path toward the Hollow Tube, and to make the top of the Tube invisible, so they'll all fall into it."

Kaliko went away shaking his head, for he thought Ruggedo was making a great mistake. He found the Magician and had the path twisted so that it led directly to the opening of the Hollow Tube, and this opening he made invisible.

Having obeyed the orders of his master, the Royal Chamberlain went to his private room and began to write letters of recommendation of himself, stating that he was an honest man, a good servant and a small eater.

"Pretty soon," he said to himself, "I shall have to look for another job, for it is certain that Ruggedo has ruined himself by this reckless defiance of the mighty Tititi-Hoochoo. And in seeking a job nothing is so effective as a letter of recommendation."

CHAPTER 10

A Terrible Tumble Through a Tube

I SUPPOSE that Polychrome, and perhaps Queen Ann and her Army, might have been able to dispel the enchantment of Ruggedo's Chief Magician had they known that danger lay in their pathway; for the Rainbow's Daughter was a fairy and as Oogaboo is a part of the Land of Oz its inhabitants cannot easily be deceived by such common magic as the Nome King could command. But no one suspected any especial danger until after they had entered Ruggedo's cavern, and so they were journeying along in quite a contented manner when Tik-Tok, who marched ahead, suddenly disappeared.

The officers thought he must have turned a corner, so they kept on their way and all of them likewise disappeared—one

107

after another. Queen Ann was rather surprised at this, and in hastening forward to learn the reason she also vanished from sight.

Betsy Bobbin had tired her feet by walking, so she was now riding upon the back of the stout little mule, facing backward and talking to Shaggy and Polychrome, who were just behind. Suddenly Hank pitched forward and began falling and Betsy would have tumbled over his head had she not grabbed the mule's shaggy neck with both arms and held on for dear life.

All around was darkness, and they were not falling directly downward but seemed to be sliding along a steep incline. Hank's hoofs were resting upon some smooth substance over which he slid with the swiftness of the wind. Once Betsy's heels flew up and struck a similar substance overhead. They were, indeed, descending the "Hollow Tube" that led to the other side of the world.

"Stop, Hank—stop!" cried the girl; but Hank only uttered a plaintive "Hee-haw!" for it was impossible for him to obey.

After several minutes had passed and no harm had befallen them, Betsy gained courage. She could see nothing at all, nor could she hear anything except the rush of air past her ears as they plunged downward along the Tube. Whether she and Hank were alone, or the others were with them, she could not tell. But had some one been able to take a flash-

Chapter Ten

light photograph of the Tube at that time a most curious picture would have resulted. There was Tik-Tok, flat upon his back and sliding headforemost down the incline. And there were the Officers of the Army of Oogaboo, all tangled up in a confused crowd, flapping their arms and trying to shield their faces from the clanking swords, which swung back and forth during the swift journey and pommeled everyone within their reach. Now followed Queen Ann, who had struck the Tube in a sitting position and went flying along with a dash and abandon that thoroughly bewildered the poor lady, who had no idea what had happened to her. Then, a little distance away, but unseen by the others in the inky darkness, slid Betsy and Hank, while behind them were Shaggy and Polychrome and finally Files and the Princess.

When first they tumbled into the Tube all were too dazed to think clearly, but the trip was a long one, because the cavity led straight through the earth to a place just opposite the Nome King's dominions, and long before the adventurers got to the end they had begun to recover their wits.

"This is awful, Hank!" cried Betsy in a loud voice, and Queen Ann heard her and called out: "Are you safe, Betsy?"

"Mercy, no!" answered the little girl. "How could anyone be safe when she's going about sixty miles a minute?" Then, after a pause, she added: "But where do you s'pose we're going to, Your Maj'sty?"

"Don't ask her that, please don't!" said Shaggy, who was not too far away to overhear them. "And please don't ask me why, either."

"Why?" said Betsy.

"No one can tell where we are going until we get there," replied Shaggy, and then he yelled "Ouch!" for Polychrome had overtaken him and was now sitting on his head.

The Rainbow's Daughter laughed merrily, and so infectious was this joyous laugh that Betsy echoed it and Hank said "Hee-haw!" in a mild and sympathetic tone of voice.

"I'd like to know where and when we'll arrive, just the same," exclaimed the little girl.

"Be patient and you'll find out, my dear," said Polychrome. "But isn't this an odd experience? Here am I, whose home is in the skies, making a journey through the center of the earth —where I never expected to be!"

"How do you know we're in the center of the earth?" asked Betsy, her voice trembling a little through nervousness.

"Why, we can't be anywhere else," replied Polychrome. "I have often heard of this passage, which was once built by a Magician who was a great traveler. He thought it would save him the bother of going around the earth's surface, but he tumbled through the Tube so fast that he shot out at the other end and hit a star in the sky, which at once exploded."

"The star exploded?" asked Betsy wonderingly.

Chapter Ten

"Yes; the Magician hit it so hard."

"And what became of the Magician?" inquired the girl.

"No one knows that," answered Polychrome. "But I don't think it matters much."

"It matters a good deal, if we also hit the stars when we come out," said Queen Ann, with a moan.

"Don't worry," advised Polychrome. "I believe the Magician was going the other way, and probably he went much faster than we are going."

"It's fast enough to suit me," remarked Shaggy, gently removing Polychrome's heel from his left eye. "Couldn't you manage to fall all by yourself, my dear?"

"I'll try," laughed the Rainbow's Daughter.

All this time they were swiftly falling through the Tube, and it was not so easy for them to talk as you may imagine when you read their words. But although they were so helpless and altogether in the dark as to their fate, the fact that they were able to converse at all cheered them considerably.

Files and Ozga were also conversing as they clung tightly to one another, and the young fellow bravely strove to reassure the Princess, although he was terribly frightened, both on her account and on his own.

An hour, under such trying circumstances, is a very long time, and for more than an hour they continued their fearful journey. Then, just as they began to fear the Tube would never end, Tik-Tok popped out into broad daylight and, after making a graceful circle in the air, fell with a splash into a great marble fountain.

Out came the officers, in quick succession, tumbling heels over head and striking the ground in many undignified attitudes.

"For the love of sassafras!" exclaimed a Peculiar Person who was hoeing pink violets in a garden. "What can all this mean?"

For answer, Queen Ann sailed up from the Tube, took a ride through the air as high as the treetops, and alighted squarely on top of the Peculiar Person's head, smashing a jeweled crown over his eyes and tumbling him to the ground.

The mule was heavier and had Betsy clinging to his back, so he did not go so high up. Fortunately for his little rider he struck the ground upon his four feet. Betsy was jarred a trifle but not hurt and when she looked around her she saw the Queen and the Peculiar Person struggling together upon the ground, where the man was trying to choke Ann and she had both hands in his bushy hair and was pulling with all her might. Some of the officers, when they got upon their feet, hastened to separate the combatants and sought to restrain the Peculiar Person so that he could not attack their Queen again.

By this time, Shaggy, Polychrome, Ozga and Files had all

arrived and were curiously examining the strange country in which they found themselves and which they knew to be exactly on the opposite side of the world from the place where they had fallen into the Tube. It was a lovely place, indeed, and seemed to be the garden of some great Prince, for through the vistas of trees and shrubbery could be seen the towers of an immense castle. But as yet the only inhabitant to greet them was the Peculiar Person just mentioned, who had shaken off the grasp of the officers without effort and was now trying to pull the battered crown from off his eyes.

Shaggy, who was always polite, helped him to do this and when the man was free and could see again he looked at his visitors with evident amazement.

"Well, well, well!" he exclaimed. "Where did you come from and how did you get here?"

Betsy tried to answer him, for Queen Ann was surly and silent.

"I can't say, exac'ly where we came from, 'cause I don't know the name of the place," said the girl, "but the way we got here was through the Hollow Tube."

"Don't call it a 'hollow' Tube, please," exclaimed the Peculiar Person in an irritated tone of voice. "If it's a tube, it's sure to be hollow."

"Why?" asked Betsy.

"Because all tubes are made that way. But this Tube is

private property and everyone is forbidden to fall into it."

"We didn't do it on purpose," explained Betsy, and Polychrome added:

"I am quite sure that Ruggedo. the Nome King, pushed us down that Tube."

"Ha! Ruggedo! Did you say Ruggedo?" cried the man, becoming much excited.

"That is what she said," replied Shaggy, "and I believe she is right. We were on our way to conquer the Nome King when suddenly we fell into the Tube."

"Then you are enemies of Ruggedo?" inquired the Peculiar Person.

"Not exac'ly enemies," said Betsy, a little puzzled by the question, "'cause we don't know him at all; but we started out to conquer him, which isn't as friendly as it might be."

"True," agreed the man. He looked thoughtfully from one to another of them for a while and then he turned his head over his shoulder and said: "Never mind the fire and pincers, my good brothers. It will be best to take these strangers to the Private Citizen."

"Very well, Tubekins," responded a Voice, deep and powerful, that seemed to come out of the air, for the speaker was invisible.

All our friends gave a jump, at this. Even Polychrome was so startled that her gauze draperies fluttered like a banner in a breeze. Shaggy shook his head and sighed; Queen Ann looked very unhappy; the officers clung to each other, trembling violently.

But soon they gained courage to look more closely at the Peculiar Person. As he was a type of all the inhabitants of this extraordinary land whom they afterward met, I will try to tell you what he looked like.

His face was beautiful, but lacked expression. His eyes were large and blue in color and his teeth finely formed and white as snow. His hair was black and bushy and seemed inclined to curl at the ends. So far no one could find any fault with his appearance. He wore a robe of scarlet, which did not cover his arms and extended no lower than his bare knees. On the bosom of the robe was embroidered a terrible dragon's head, as horrible to look at as the man was beautiful. His arms and legs were left bare and the skin of one arm was bright yellow and the skin of the other arm a vivid green. He had one blue leg and one pink one, while both his feet—which showed through the open sandals he wore—were jet black.

Betsy could not decide whether these gorgeous colors were dyes or the natural tints of the skin, but while she was thinking it over the man who had been called "Tubekins" said:

"Follow me to the Residence—all of you!"

But just then a Voice exclaimed: "Here's another of them, Tubekins, lying in the water of the fountain."

"Gracious!" cried Betsy; "it must be Tik-Tok, and he'll drown."

"Water is a bad thing for his clockworks, anyhow," agreed Shaggy, as with one accord they all started for the fountain. But before they could reach it, invisible hands raised Tik-Tok from the marble basin and set him upon his feet beside it, water dripping from every joint of his copper body.

"Ma—ny tha—tha—tha—thanks!" he said; and then his copper jaws clicked together and he could say no more. He next made an attempt to walk but after several awkward trials found he could not move his joints.

Peals of jeering laughter from persons unseen greeted Tik-Tok's failure, and the new arrivals in this strange land found it very uncomfortable to realize that there were many creatures around them who were invisible, yet could be heard plainly.

"Shall I wind him up?" asked Betsy, feeling very sorry for Tik-Tok.

"I think his machinery is wound; but he needs oiling," replied Shaggy.

At once an oil-can appeared before him, held on a level with his eyes by some unseen hand. Shaggy took the can and tried to oil Tik-Tok's joints. As if to assist him, a strong current of warm air was directed against the copper man, which quickly dried him. Soon he was able to say "Ma-ny thanks!"

quite smoothly and his joints worked fairly well.

"Come!" commanded Tubekins, and turning his back upon them he walked up the path toward the castle.

"Shall we go?" asked Queen Ann, uncertainly; but just then she received a shove that almost pitched her forward on her head; so she decided to go. The officers who hesitated received several energetic kicks, but could not see who delivered them; therefore they also decided—very wisely—to go. The others followed willingly enough, for unless they ventured upon another terrible journey through the Tube they must make the best of the unknown country they were in, and the best seemed to be to obey orders.

CHAPTER 11

The Famous Fellowship of Fairies

AFTER a short walk through very beautiful gardens they came to the castle and followed Tubekins through the entrance and into a great domed chamber, where he commanded them to be seated.

From the crown which he wore, Betsy had thought this man must be the King of the country they were in, yet after he had seated all the strangers upon benches that were ranged in a semicircle before a high throne, Tubekins bowed humbly before the vacant throne and in a flash became invisible and disappeared.

The hall was an immense place, but there seemed to be no one in it beside themselves. Presently, however, they heard a low cough near them, and here and there was the faint rustling of a robe and a slight patter as of footsteps. Then suddenly there rang out the clear tone of a bell and at the sound all was changed.

Gazing around the hall in bewilderment they saw that it was filled with hundreds of men and women, all with beautiful faces and staring blue eyes and all wearing scarlet robes and jeweled crowns upon their heads. In fact, these people seemed exact duplicates of Tubekins and it was difficult to find any mark by which to tell them apart.

"My! what a lot of Kings and Queens!" whispered Betsy to Polychrome, who sat beside her and appeared much interested in the scene but not a bit worried.

"It is certainly a strange sight," was Polychrome's reply; "but I cannot see how there can be more than one King, or Queen, in any one country, for were these all rulers, no one could tell who was Master."

One of the Kings who stood near and overheard this remark turned to her and said: "One who is Master of himself is always a King, if only to himself. In this favored land all Kings and Queens are equal, and it is our privilege to bow before one supreme Ruler—the Private Citizen."

"Who's he?" inquired Betsy.

As if to answer her, the clear tones of the bell again rang out and instantly there appeared seated in the throne the man who was lord and master of all these royal ones. This fact was evident when with one accord they fell upon their knees and touched their foreheads to the floor.

The Private Citizen was not unlike the others, except that his eyes were black instead of blue and in the centers of the black irises glowed red sparks that seemed like coals of fire. But his features were very beautiful and dignified and his manner composed and stately. Instead of the prevalent scarlet robe, he wore one of white, and the same dragon's head that decorated the others was embroidered upon its bosom.

"What charge lies against these people, Tubekins?" he asked in quiet, even tones.

"They came through the forbidden Tube, O Mighty Citizen," was the reply.

"You see, it was this way," said Betsy. "We were marching to the Nome King, to conquer him and set Shaggy's brother free, when on a sudden—"

"Who are you?" demanded the Private Citizen sternly.

"Me? Oh, I'm Betsy Bobbin, and—"

"Who is the leader of this party?" asked the Citizen.

"Sir, I am Queen Ann of Oogaboo, and—"

"Then keep quiet," said the Citizen. "Who is the leader?"

No one answered for a moment. Then General Bunn stood up.

"Sit down!" commanded the Citizen. "I can see that sixteen of you are merely officers, and of no account."

"But we have an Army," said General Clock, blusteringly, for he didn't like to be told he was of no account.

"Where is your Army?" asked the Citizen.

"It's me," said Tik-Tok, his voice sounding a little rusty. "I'm the on-ly Pri-vate Sol-dier in the par-ty."

Hearing this, the Citizen rose and bowed respectfully to the Clockwork Man.

"Pardon me for not realizing your importance before," said he. "Will you oblige me by taking a seat beside me on my throne?"

Tik-Tok rose and walked over to the throne, all the Kings and Queens making way for him. Then with clanking steps he mounted the platform and sat on the broad seat beside the Citizen.

Ann was greatly provoked at this mark of favor shown to the humble Clockwork Man, but Shaggy seemed much pleased that his old friend's importance had been recognized by the ruler of this remarkable country. The Citizen now began to question Tik-Tok, who told in his mechanical voice about Shaggy's quest of his lost brother, and how Ozma of Oz had sent the Clockwork Man to assist him, and how they had fallen in with Queen Ann and her people from Oogaboo. Also he told how Betsy and Hank and Polychrome and the Rose Princess had happened to join their party.

"And you intended to conquer Ruggedo, the Metal Monarch and King of the Nomes?" asked the Citizen.

"Yes. That seemed the on-ly thing for us to do," was Tik-Tok's reply. "But he was too clev-er for us. When we got close to his cav-ern he made our path lead to the Tube, and made the op-en-ing in-vis-i-ble, so that we all fell in-to it be-fore we knew it was there. It was an eas-y way to get rid of us and now Rug-ge-do is safe and we are far a-way in a strange land."

The Citizen was silent a moment and seemed to be thinking. Then he said:

"Most noble Private Soldier, I must inform you that by the laws of our country anyone who comes through the Forbidden Tube must be tortured for nine days and ten nights and then thrown back into the Tube. But it is wise to disregard laws when they conflict with justice, and it seems that you and your followers did not disobey our laws willingly, being forced into the Tube by Ruggedo. Therefore the Nome King is alone to blame, and he alone must be punished."

"That suits me," said Tik-Tok. "But Rug-ge-do is on the o-ther side of the world where he is a-way out of your reach."

The Citizen drew himself up proudly.

"Do you imagine anything in the world or upon it can be out of the reach of the Great Jinjin?" he asked.

Chapter Eleven

"Oh! Are you, then, the Great Jinjin?" inquired Tik-Tok.

"I am."

"Then your name is Ti-ti-ti-Hoo-choo?"

"It is."

Queen Ann gave a scream and began to tremble. Shaggy was so disturbed that he took out a handkerchief and wiped the perspiration from his brow. Polychrome looked sober and uneasy for the first time, while Files put his arms around the Rose Princess as if to protect her. As for the officers, the name of the great Jinjin set them moaning and weeping at a great rate and every one fell upon his knees before the throne, begging for mercy. Betsy was worried at seeing her companions so disturbed, but did not know what it was all about. Only Tik-Tok was unmoved at the discovery.

"Then," said he, "if you are Ti-ti-ti-Hoo-choo, and think Rug-ge-do is to blame, I am sure that some-thing queer will hap-pen to the King of the Nomes."

"I wonder what 'twill be," said Betsy.

The Private Citizen—otherwise known as Tititi-Hoochoo, the Great Jinjin—looked at the little girl steadily.

"I will presently decide what is to happen to Ruggedo," said he in a hard, stern voice. Then, turning to the throng of Kings and Queens, he continued: "Tik-Tok has spoken truly, for his machinery will not allow him to lie, nor will it allow

125

his thoughts to think falsely. Therefore these people are not our enemies and must be treated with consideration and justice. Take them to your palaces and entertain them as guests until to-morrow, when I command that they be brought again to my Residence. By then I shall have formed my plans."

No sooner had Tititi-Hoochoo spoken than he disappeared from sight. Immediately after, most of the Kings and Queens likewise disappeared. But several of them remained visible and approached the strangers with great respect. One of the lovely Queens said to Betsy:

"I trust you will honor me by being my guest. I am Erma, Queen of Light."

"May Hank come with me?" asked the girl.

"The King of Animals will care for your mule," was the reply. "But do not fear for him, for he will be treated royally. All of your party will be reunited on the morrow."

"I—I'd like to have *some* one with me," said Betsy, pleadingly.

Queen Erma looked around and smiled upon Polychrome.

"Will the Rainbow's Daughter be an agreeable companion?" she asked.

"Oh, yes!" exclaimed the girl.

So Polychrome and Betsy became guests of the Queen of Light, while other beautiful Kings and Queens took charge of the others of the party.

The two girls followed Erma out of the hall and through the gardens of the Residence to a village of pretty dwellings. None of these was so large or imposing as the castle of the Private Citizen, but all were handsome enough to be called palaces—as, in fact, they really were.

CHAPTER 12

The Lovely Lady of Light

THE PALACE of the Queen of Light stood on a little eminence and was a mass of crystal windows, surmounted by a vast crystal dome. When they entered the portals Erma was greeted by six lovely maidens, evidently of high degree, who at once aroused Betsy's admiration. Each bore a wand in her hand, tipped with an emblem of light, and their costumes were also emblematic of the lights they represented. Erma introduced them to her guests and each made a graceful and courteous acknowledgment.

First was Sunlight, radiantly beautiful and very fair; the second was Moonlight, a soft, dreamy damsel with nut-brown hair; next came Starlight, equally lovely but inclined to be retiring and shy. These three were dressed in shimmering

129

robes of silvery white. The fourth was Daylight, a brilliant damsel with laughing eyes and frank manners, who wore a variety of colors. Then came Firelight, clothed in a fleecy flame-colored robe that wavered around her shapely form in a very attractive manner. The sixth maiden, Electra, was the most beautiful of all, and Betsy thought from the first that both Sunlight and Daylight regarded Electra with envy and were a little jealous of her.

But all were cordial in their greetings to the strangers and seemed to regard the Queen of Light with much affection, for they fluttered around her in a flashing, radiant group as she led the way to her regal drawing-room.

This apartment was richly and cosily furnished, the upholstery being of many tints, and both Betsy and Polychrome enjoyed resting themselves upon the downy divans after their strenuous adventures of the day.

The Queen sat down to chat with her guests, who noticed that Daylight was the only maiden now seated beside Erma. The others had retired to another part of the room, where they sat modestly with entwined arms and did not intrude themselves at all.

The Queen told the strangers all about this beautiful land, which is one of the chief residences of fairies who minister to the needs of mankind. So many important fairies lived

Chapter Twelve

there that, to avoid rivalry, they had elected as their Ruler the only important personage in the country who had no duties to mankind to perform and was, in effect, a Private Citizen. This Ruler, or Jinjin, as was his title, bore the name of Tititi-Hoochoo, and the most singular thing about him was that he had no heart. But instead of this he possessed a high degree of Reason and Justice and while he showed no mercy in his judgments he never punished unjustly or without reason. To wrong-doers Tititi-Hoochoo was as terrible as he was heartless, but those who were innocent of evil had nothing to fear from him.

All the Kings and Queens of this fairyland paid reverence to Jinjin, for as they expected to be obeyed by others they were willing to obey the one in authority over them.

The inhabitants of the Land of Oz had heard many tales of this fearfully just Jinjin, whose punishments were always equal to the faults committed. Polychrome also knew of him, although this was the first time she had ever seen him face to face. But to Betsy the story was all new, and she was greatly interested in Tititi-Hoochoo, whom she no longer feared.

Time sped swiftly during their talk and suddenly Betsy noticed that Moonlight was sitting beside the Queen of Light, instead of Daylight.

"But tell me, please," she pleaded, "why do you all wear a dragon's head embroidered on your gowns?"

Erma's pleasant face became grave as she answered:

"The Dragon, as you must know, was the first living creature ever made; therefore the Dragon is the oldest and wisest of living things. By good fortune the Original Dragon, who still lives, is a resident of this land and supplies us with wisdom whenever we are in need of it. He is old as the world and remembers everything that has happened since the world was created."

"Did he ever have any children?" inquired the girl.

"Yes, many of them. Some wandered into other lands, where men, not understanding them, made war upon them; but many still reside in this country. None, however, is as wise as the Original Dragon, for whom we have great respect. As he was the first resident here, we wear the emblem of the dragon's head to show that we are the favored people who alone have the right to inhabit this fairyland, which in beauty almost equal the Fairyland of Oz, and in power quite surpasses it."

"I understand about the dragon, now," said Polychrome, nodding her lovely head. Betsy did not quite understand, but she was at present interested in observing the changing lights. As Daylight had given way to Moonlight, so now Starlight sat at the right hand of Erma the Queen, and with her coming a spirit of peace and content seemed to fill the room. Polychrome, being herself a fairy, had many questions

Chapter Twelve

to ask about the various Kings and Queens who lived in this far-away, secluded place, and before Erma had finished answering them a rosy glow filled the room and Firelight took her place beside the Queen.

Betsy liked Firelight, but to gaze upon her warm and glowing features made the little girl sleepy, and presently she began to nod. Thereupon Erma rose and took Betsy's hand gently in her own.

"Come," said she; "the feast time has arrived and the feast is spread."

"That's nice," exclaimed the small mortal. "Now that I think of it, I'm awful hungry. But p'raps I can't eat your fairy food."

The Queen smiled and led her to a doorway. As she pushed aside a heavy drapery a flood of silvery light greeted them, and Betsy saw before her a splendid banquet hall, with a table spread with snowy linen and crystal and silver. At one side was a broad, throne-like seat for Erma and beside her now sat the brilliant maid Electra. Polychrome was placed on the Queen's right hand and Betsy upon her left. The other five messengers of light now waited upon them, and each person was supplied with just the food she liked best. Polychrome found her dish of dewdrops, all fresh and sparkling, while Betsy was so lavishly served that she decided she had never in her life eaten a dinner half so good.

"I s'pose," she said to the Queen, "that Miss Electra is the youngest of all these girls."

"Why do you suppose that?" inquired Erma, with a smile.

"'Cause electric'ty is the newest light we know of. Didn't Mr. Edison discover it?"

"Perhaps he was the first mortal to discover it," replied the Queen. "But electricity was a part of the world from its creation, and therefore my Electra is as old as Daylight or Moonlight, and equally beneficent to mortals and fairies alike."

Betsy was thoughtful for a time. Then she remarked, as she looked at the six messengers of light:

"We couldn't very well do without any of 'em; could we?"

Erma laughed softly. "*I* couldn't, I'm sure," she replied, "and I think mortals would miss any one of my maidens, as well. Daylight cannot take the place of Sunlight, which gives us strength and energy. Moonlight is of value when Daylight, worn out with her long watch, retires to rest. If the moon in its course is hidden behind the earth's rim, and my sweet Moonlight cannot cheer us, Starlight takes her place, for the skies always lend her power. Without Firelight we should miss much of our warmth and comfort, as well as much cheer when the walls of houses encompass us. But always, when other lights forsake us, our glorious Electra is ready to flood us with bright rays. As Queen of Light, I love all my maidens, for I know them to be faithful and true."

"I love 'em, too!" declared Betsy. "But sometimes, when I'm *real* sleepy, I can get along without any light at all."

"Are you sleepy now?" inquired Erma, for the feast had ended.

"A little," admitted the girl.

So Electra showed her to a pretty chamber where there was a soft, white bed, and waited patiently until Betsy had undressed and put on a shimmery silken nightrobe that lay beside her pillow. Then the light-maid bade her good night and opened the door.

When she closed it after her Betsy was in darkness. In six winks the little girl was fast asleep.

CHAPTER 13

The Jinjin's Just Judgment

ALL the adventurers were reunited next morning when they were brought from various palaces to the Residence of Tititi-Hoochoo and ushered into the great Hall of State.

As before, no one was visible except our friends and their escorts until the first bell sounded. Then in a flash the room was seen to be filled with the beautiful Kings and Queens of the land. The second bell marked the appearance in the throne of the mighty Jinjin, whose handsome countenance was as composed and expressionless as ever.

All bowed low to the Ruler. Their voices softly murmured: "We greet the Private Citizen, mightiest of Rulers, whose word is Law and whose Law is just."

Chapter Thirteen

Tititi-Hoochoo bowed in acknowledgment. Then, looking around the brilliant assemblage, and at the little group of adventurers before him, he said:

"An unusual thing has happened. Inhabitants of other lands than ours, who are different from ourselves in many ways, have been thrust upon us through the Forbidden Tube, which one of our people foolishly made years ago and was properly punished for his folly. But these strangers had no desire to come here and were wickedly thrust into the Tube by a cruel King on the other side of the world, named Ruggedo. This King is an immortal, but he is not good. His magic powers hurt mankind more than they benefit them. Because he had unjustly kept the Shaggy Man's brother a prisoner, this little band of honest people, consisting of both mortals and immortals, determined to conquer Ruggedo and to punish him. Fearing they might succeed in this, the Nome King misled them so that they fell into the Tube.

"Now, this same Ruggedo has been warned by me, many times, that if ever he used this Forbidden Tube in any way he would be severely punished. I find, by referring to the Fairy Records, that this King's servant, a nome named Kaliko, begged his master not to do such a wrong act as to drop these people into the Tube and send them tumbling into our country. But Ruggedo defied me and my orders.

"Therefore these strangers are innocent of any wrong. It

137

is only Ruggedo who deserves punishment, and I will punish him." He paused a moment and then continued in the same cold, merciless voice:

"These strangers must return through the Tube to their own side of the world; but I will make their fall more easy and pleasant than it was before. Also I shall send with them an Instrument of Vengeance, who in my name will drive Ruggedo from his underground caverns, take away his magic powers and make him a homeless wanderer on the face of the earth—a place he detests."

There was a little murmur of horror from the Kings and Queens at the severity of this punishment, but no one uttered a protest, for all realized that the sentence was just.

"In selecting my Instrument of Vengeance," went on Tititi-Hoochoo, "I have realized that this will be an unpleasant mission. Therefore no one of us who is blameless should be forced to undertake it. In this wonderful land it is seldom one is guilty of wrong, even in the slightest degree, and on examining the Records I found no King or Queen had erred. Nor had any among their followers or servants done any wrong. But finally I came to the Dragon Family, which we highly respect, and then it was that I discovered the error of Quox.

"Quox, as you well know, is a young dragon who has not yet acquired the wisdom of his race. Because of this lack, he has been disrespectful toward his most ancient ancestor, the Original Dragon, telling him once to mind his own business and again saying that the Ancient One had grown foolish with age. We are aware that dragons are not the same as fairies and cannot be altogether guided by our laws, yet such disrespect as Quox has shown should not be unnoticed by us. Therefore I have selected Quox as my royal Instrument of Vengeance and he shall go through the Tube with these people and inflict upon Ruggedo the punishment I have decreed."

All had listened quietly to this speech and now the Kings and Queens bowed gravely to signify their approval of the Jinjin's judgment.

Tititi-Hoochoo turned to Tubekins.

"I command you," said he, "to escort these strangers to the Tube and see that they all enter it."

The King of the Tube, who had first discovered our friends and brought them to the Private Citizen, stepped forward and bowed. As he did so, the Jinjin and all the Kings and Queens suddenly disappeared and only Tubekins remained visible.

"All right," said Betsy, with a sigh; "I don't mind going back so *very* much, 'cause the Jinjin promised to make it easy for us."

Indeed, Queen Ann and her officers were the only ones who looked solemn and seemed to fear the return journey.

139

One thing that bothered Ann was her failure to conquer this land of Tititi-Hoochoo. As they followed their guide through the gardens to the mouth of the Tube she said to Shaggy:

"How can I conquer the world, if I go away and leave this rich country unconquered?"

"You can't," he replied. "Don't ask me why, please, for if you don't know I can't inform you."

"Why not?" said Ann; but Shaggy paid no attention to the question.

This end of the Tube had a silver rim and around it was a gold railing to which was attached a sign that read:

"IF YOU ARE OUT, STAY THERE.
IF YOU ARE IN, DON'T COME OUT."

On a little silver plate just inside the Tube was engraved the words:

" *Burrowed and built by*
Hiergargo the Magician,
In the Year of the World
1 9 6 2 5 4 7 8
For his own exclusive uses."

"He was some builder, I must say," remarked Betsy, when

she had read the inscription; "but if he had known about that star I guess he'd have spent his time playing solitaire."

"Well, what are we waiting for?" inquired Shaggy, who was impatient to start.

"Quox," replied Tubekins. "But I think I hear him coming."

"Is the young dragon invisible?" asked Ann, who had never seen a live dragon and was a little fearful of meeting one.

"No, indeed," replied the King of the Tube. "You'll see him in a minute; but before you part company I'm sure you'll wish he *was* invisible."

"Is he dangerous, then?" questioned Files.

"Not at all. But Quox tires me dreadfully," said Tubekins, "and I prefer his room to his company."

At that instant a scraping sound was heard, drawing nearer and nearer until from between two big bushes appeared a huge dragon, who approached the party, nodded his head and said: "Good morning."

Had Quox been at all bashful I am sure he would have felt uncomfortable at the astonished stare of every eye in the group—except Tubekins, of course, who was not astonished because he had seen Quox so often.

Betsy had thought a "young" dragon must be a small dragon, yet here was one so enormous that the girl decided he must be full grown, if not overgrown. His body was a lovely sky-blue in color and it was thickly set with glittering silver scales, each one as big as a serving-tray. Around his neck was a pink ribbon with a bow just under his left ear, and below the ribbon appeared a chain of pearls to which was attached a golden locket about as large around as the end of a bass drum. This locket was set with many large and beautiful jewels.

The head and face of Quox were not especially ugly, when you consider that he was a dragon; but his eyes were so large that it took him a long time to wink and his teeth seemed very sharp and terrible when they showed, which they did whenever the beast smiled. Also his nostrils were quite large and wide, and those who stood near him were liable to smell brimstone—especially when he breathed out fire, as it is the nature of dragons to do. To the end of his long tail was attached a big electric light.

Perhaps the most singular thing about the dragon's appearance at this time was the fact that he had a row of seats attached to his back, one seat for each member of the party. These seats were double, with curved backs, so that two could sit in them, and there were twelve of these double seats, all strapped firmly around the dragon's thick body and placed one behind the other, in a row that extended from his shoulders nearly to his tail.

Chapter Thirteen

"Aha!" exclaimed Tubekins; "I see that Tititi-Hoochoo has transformed Quox into a carryall."

"I'm glad of that," said Betsy. "I hope, Mr. Dragon, you won't mind our riding on your back."

"Not a bit," replied Quox. "I'm in disgrace just now, you know, and the only way to redeem my good name is to obey the orders of the Jinjin. If he makes me a beast of burden, it is only a part of my punishment, and I must bear it like a dragon. I don't blame you people at all, and I hope you'll enjoy the ride. Hop on, please. All aboard for the other side of the world!"

Silently they took their places. Hank sat in the front seat with Betsy, so that he could rest his front hoofs upon the dragon's head. Behind them were Shaggy and Polychrome, then Files and the Princess, and Queen Ann and Tik-Tok. The officers rode in the rear seats. When all had mounted to their places the dragon looked very like one of those sight-seeing wagons so common in big cities—only he had legs instead of wheels.

"All ready?" asked Quox, and when they said they were he crawled to the mouth of the Tube and put his head in.

"Good-bye, and good luck to you!" called Tubekins; but no one thought to reply, because just then the dragon slid his great body into the Tube and the journey to the other side of the world had begun.

143

At first they went so fast that they could scarcely catch their breaths, but presently Quox slowed up and said with a sort of cackling laugh:

"My scales! but that is some tumble. I think I shall take it easy and fall slower, or I'm likely to get dizzy. Is it very far to the other side of the world?"

"Haven't you ever been through this Tube before?" inquired Shaggy.

"Never. Nor has anyone else in our country; at least, not since I was born."

"How long ago was that?" asked Betsy.

"That I was born? Oh, not very long ago. I'm only a mere child. If I had not been sent on this journey, I would have celebrated my three thousand and fifty-sixth birthday next Thursday. Mother was going to make me a birthday cake with three thousand and fifty-six candles on it; but now, of course, there will be no celebration, for I fear I shall not get home in time for it."

"Three thousand and fifty-six years!" cried Betsy. "Why, I had no idea anything could live that long!"

"My respected Ancestor, whom I would call a stupid old humbug if I had not reformed, is so old that I am a mere baby compared with him," said Quox. "He dates from the beginning of the world, and insists on telling us stories of things that happened fifty thousand years ago, which are of no inter-

Chapter Thirteen

est at all to youngsters like me. In fact, Grandpa isn't up to date. He lives altogether in the past, so I can't see any good reason for his being alive to-day. . . . Are you people able to see your way, or shall I turn on more light?"

"Oh, we can see very nicely, thank you; only there's nothing to see but ourselves," answered Betsy.

This was true. The dragon's big eyes were like headlights on an automobile and illuminated the Tube far ahead of them. Also he curled his tail upward so that the electric light on the end of it enabled them to see one another quite clearly. But the Tube itself was only dark metal, smooth as glass but exactly the same from one of its ends to the other. Therefore there was no scenery of interest to beguile the journey.

They were now falling so gently that the trip was proving entirely comfortable, as the Jinjin had promised it would be; but this meant a longer journey and the only way they could make time pass was to engage in conversation. The dragon seemed a willing and persistent talker and he was of so much interest to them that they encouraged him to chatter. His voice was a little gruff but not unpleasant when one became used to it.

"My only fear," said he presently, "is that this constant sliding over the surface of the Tube will dull my claws. You see, this hole isn't straight down, but on a steep slant, and so instead of tumbling freely through the air I must skate along the Tube. Fortunately, there is a file in my tool-kit, and if my claws get dull they can be sharpened again."

"Why do you want sharp claws?" asked Betsy.

"They are my natural weapons, and you must not forget that I have been sent to conquer Ruggedo."

"Oh, you needn't mind about that," remarked Queen Ann, in her most haughty manner; "for when we get to Ruggedo I and my invincible Army can conquer him without your assistance."

"Very good," returned the dragon, cheerfully. "That will save me a lot of bother—if you succeed. But I think I shall file my claws, just the same."

He gave a long sigh, as he said this, and a sheet of flame, several feet in length, shot from his mouth. Betsy shuddered and Hank said "Hee-haw!" while some of the officers screamed in terror. But the dragon did not notice that he had done anything unusual.

"Is there fire inside of you?" asked Shaggy.

"Of course," answered Quox. "What sort of a dragon would I be if my fire went out?"

"What keeps it going?" Betsy inquired.

"I've no idea. I only know it's there," said Quox. "The fire keeps me alive and enables me to move; also to think and speak."

Chapter Thirteen

"Ah! You are ver-y much like my-self," said Tik-Tok. "The on-ly dif-fer-ence is that I move by clock-work, while you move by fire."

"I don't see a particle of likeness between us, I must con-fess," retorted Quox, gruffly. "You are not a live thing; you're a dummy."

"But I can do things, you must ad-mit," said Tik-Tok.

"Yes, when you are wound up," sneered the dragon. "But if you run down, you are helpless."

"What would happen to you, Quox, if you ran out of gasoline?" inquired Shaggy, who did not like this attack upon his friend.

"I don't use gasoline."

"Well, suppose you ran out of fire."

"What's the use of supposing that?" asked Quox. "My great-great-great-grandfather has lived since the world began, and he has never once run out of fire to keep him going. But I will confide to you that as he gets older he shows more smoke and less fire. As for Tik-Tok, he's well enough in his way, but he's merely copper. And the Metal Monarch knows copper through and through. I wouldn't be surprised if Ruggedo melted Tik-Tok in one of his furnaces and made copper pennies of him."

"In that case, I would still keep going," remarked Tik-Tok, calmly.

147

"Pennies do," said Betsy regretfully.

"This is all nonsense," said the Queen, with irritation. "Tik-Tok is my great Army—all but the officers—and I believe he will be able to conquer Ruggedo with ease. What do you think, Polychrome?"

"You might let him try," answered the Rainbow's Daughter, with her sweet ringing laugh, that sounded like the tinkling of tiny bells. "And if Tik-Tok fails, you have still the big fire-breathing dragon to fall back on."

"Ah!" said the dragon, another sheet of flame gushing from his mouth and nostrils; "it's a wise little girl, this Polychrome. Anyone would know she is a fairy."

CHAPTER 14

The Long-Eared Hearer Learns by Listening

DURING this time Ruggedo, the Metal Monarch and King of the Nomes, was trying to amuse himself in his splendid jeweled cavern. It was hard work for Ruggedo to find amusement to-day, for all the nomes were behaving well and there was no one to scold or to punish. The King had thrown his sceptre at Kaliko six times, without hitting him once. Not that Kaliko had done anything wrong. On the contrary, he had obeyed the King in every way but one: he would not stand still, when commanded to do so, and let the heavy sceptre strike him.

We can hardly blame Kaliko for this, and even the cruel Ruggedo forgave him; for he knew very well that if he

149

mashed his Royal Chamberlain he could never find another
so intelligent and obedient.   Kaliko could make the nomes
work when their King could not, for the nomes hated Ruggedo
and there were so many thousands of the quaint little underground people that they could easily have rebelled and defied
the King had they dared to do so.   Sometimes, when Ruggedo
abused them worse than usual, they grew sullen and threw
down their hammers and picks.   Then, however hard the
King scolded or whipped them, they would not work until
Kaliko came and begged them to.   For Kaliko was one of
themselves and was as much abused by the King as any nome
in the vast series of caverns.

But to-day all the little people were working indus-
triously at their tasks and Ruggedo, having nothing to do,
was greatly bored.   He sent for the Long-Eared Hearer and
asked him to listen carefully and report what was going on in
the big world.

"It seems," said the Hearer, after listening for awhile,
"that the women in America have clubs."

"Are there spikes in them?" asked Ruggedo, yawning.

"I cannot hear any spikes, Your Majesty," was the reply.

"Then their clubs are not as good as my sceptre.   What
else do you hear?"

"There's a war."

"Bah! there's always a war.   What else?"

150

Chapter Fourteen

For a time the Hearer was silent, bending forward and spreading out his big ears to catch the slightest sound. Then suddenly he said:

"Here is an interesting thing, Your Majesty. These people are arguing as to who shall conquer the Metal Monarch, seize his treasure and drive him from his dominions."

"What people?" demanded Ruggedo, sitting up straight in his throne.

"The ones you threw down the Hollow Tube."

"Where are they now?"

"In the same Tube, and coming back this way," said the Hearer.

Ruggedo got out of his throne and began to pace up and down the cavern.

"I wonder what can be done to stop them," he mused.

"Well," said the Hearer, "if you could turn the Tube upside down, they would be falling the other way, Your Majesty."

Ruggedo glared at him wickedly, for it was impossible to turn the Tube upside down and he believed the Hearer was slyly poking fun at him. Presently he asked:

"How far away are those people now?"

"About nine thousand three hundred and six miles, seventeen furlongs, eight feet and four inches—as nearly as I can

151

judge from the sound of their voices," replied the Hearer.

"Aha! Then it will be some time before they arrive," said Ruggedo, "and when they get here I shall be ready to receive them."

He rushed to his gong and pounded upon it so fiercely that Kaliko came bounding into the cavern with one shoe off and one shoe on, for he was just dressing himself after a swim in the hot bubbling lake of the Underground Kingdom.

"Kaliko, those invaders whom we threw down the Tube are coming back again!" he exclaimed.

"I thought they would," said the Royal Chamberlain, pulling on the other shoe. "Tititi-Hoochoo would not allow them to remain in his kingdom, of course, and so I've been expecting them back for some time. That was a very foolish action of yours, Rug."

"What, to throw them down the Tube?"

"Yes. Tititi-Hoochoo has forbidden us to throw even rubbish into the Tube."

"Pooh! what do I care for the Jinjin?" asked Ruggedo scornfully. "He never leaves his own kingdom, which is on the other side of the world."

"True; but he might send some one through the Tube to punish you," suggested Kaliko.

"I'd like to see him do it! Who could conquer my thousands of nomes?"

Chapter Fourteen

"Why, they've been conquered before, if I remember aright," answered Kaliko with a grin. "Once I saw you running from a little girl named Dorothy, and her friends, as if you were really afraid."

"Well, I *was* afraid, that time," admitted the Nome King, with a deep sigh, "for Dorothy had a Yellow Hen that laid eggs!"

The King shuddered as he said "eggs," and Kaliko also shuddered, and so did the Long-Eared Hearer; for eggs are the only things that the nomes greatly dread. The reason for this is that eggs belong on the earth's surface, where birds and fowl of all sorts live, and there is something about a hen's egg, especially, that fills a nome with horror. If by chance the inside of an egg touches one of these underground people, he withers up and blows away and that is the end of him— unless he manages quickly to speak a magical word which only a few of the nomes know. Therefore Ruggedo and his followers had very good cause to shudder at the mere mention of eggs.

"But Dorothy," said the King, "is not with this band of invaders; nor is the Yellow Hen. As for Tititi-Hoochoo, he has no means of knowing that we are afraid of eggs."

"You mustn't be too sure of that," Kaliko warned him. "Tititi-Hoochoo knows a great many things, being a fairy, and his powers are far superior to any we can boast."

Ruggedo shrugged impatiently and turned to the Hearer.

"Listen," said he, "and tell me if you hear any eggs coming through the Tube."

The Long-Eared one listened and then shook his head. But Kaliko laughed at the King.

"No one can hear an egg, Your Majesty," said he. "The only way to discover the truth is to look through the Magic Spyglass."

"That's it!" cried the King. "Why didn't I think of it before? Look at once, Kaliko!"

So Kaliko went to the Spyglass and by uttering a mumbled charm he caused the other end of it to twist around, so that it pointed down the opening of the Tube. Then he put his eye to the glass and was able to gaze along all the turns and windings of the Magic Spyglass and then deep into the Tube, to where our friends were at that time falling.

"Dear me!" he exclaimed. "Here comes a dragon."

"A big one?" asked Ruggedo.

"A monster. He has an electric light on the end of his tail, so I can see him very plainly. And the other people are all riding upon his back."

"How about the eggs?" inquired the King.

Kaliko looked again.

"I can see no eggs at all," said he; "but I imagine that the dragon is as dangerous as eggs. Probably Tititi-Hoochoo has

sent him here to punish you for dropping those strangers into the Forbidden Tube. I warned you not to do it, Your Majesty."

This news made the Nome King anxious. For a few minutes he paced up and down, stroking his long beard and thinking with all his might. After this he turned to Kaliko and said:

"All the harm a dragon can do is to scratch with his claws and bite with his teeth."

"That is not all, but it's quite enough," returned Kaliko earnestly. "On the other hand, no one can hurt a dragon, because he's the toughest creature alive. One flop of his huge tail could smash a hundred nomes to pancakes, and with teeth and claws he could tear even you or me into small bits, so that it would be almost impossible to put us together again. Once, a few hundred years ago, while wandering through some deserted caverns, I came upon a small piece of a nome lying on the rocky floor. I asked the piece of nome what had happened to it. Fortunately the mouth was a part of this piece—the mouth and the left eye—so it was able to tell me that a fierce dragon was the cause. It had attacked the poor nome and scattered him in every direction, and as there was no friend near to collect his pieces and put him together, they had been separated for a great many years. So you see, Your Majesty, it is not in good taste to sneer at a dragon."

Chapter Fourteen

The King had listened attentively to Kaliko. Said he:

"It will only be necessary to chain this dragon which Tititi-Hoochoo has sent here, in order to prevent his reaching us with his claws and teeth."

"He also breathes flames," Kaliko reminded him.

"My nomes are not afraid of fire, nor am I," said Ruggedo.

"Well, how about the Army of Oogaboo?"

"Sixteen cowardly officers and Tik-Tok! Why, I could defeat them single-handed; but I won't try to. I'll summon my army of nomes to drive the invaders out of my territory, and if we catch any of them I intend to stick needles into them until they hop with pain."

"I hope you won't hurt any of the girls," said Kaliko.

"I'll hurt 'em all!" roared the angry Metal Monarch. "And that braying Mule I'll make into hoof-soup, and feed it to my nomes, that it may add to their strength."

"Why not be good to the strangers and release your prisoner, the Shaggy Man's brother?" suggested Kaliko.

"Never!"

"It may save you a lot of annoyance. And you don't want the Ugly One."

"I don't want him; that's true. But I won't allow anybody to order me around. I'm King of the Nomes and I'm the Metal Monarch, and I shall do as I please and what I please and when I please!"

With this speech Ruggedo threw his sceptre at Kaliko's head, aiming it so well that the Royal Chamberlain had to fall flat upon the floor in order to escape it. But the Hearer did not see the sceptre coming and it swept past his head so closely that it broke off the tip of one of his long ears. He gave a dreadful yell that quite startled Ruggedo, and the King was sorry for the accident because those long ears of the Hearer were really valuable to him.

So the Nome King forgot to be angry with Kaliko and ordered his Chamberlain to summon General Guph and the army of nomes and have them properly armed. They were then to march to the mouth of the Tube, where they could seize the travelers as soon as they appeared.

CHAPTER 15

The Dragon Defies Danger

ALTHOUGH the journey through the Tube was longer, this time, than before, it was so much more comfortable that none of our friends minded it at all. They talked together most of the time and as they found the dragon good-natured and fond of the sound of his own voice they soon became well acquainted with him and accepted him as a companion.

"You see," said Shaggy, in his frank way, "Quox is on our side, and therefore the dragon is a good fellow. If he happened to be an enemy, instead of a friend, I am sure I should dislike him very much, for his breath smells of brimstone, he is very conceited and he is so strong and fierce that he would prove a dangerous foe."

"Yes, indeed," returned Quox, who had listened to this speech with pleasure; "I suppose I am about as terrible as any living thing. I am glad you find me conceited, for that proves I know my good qualities. As for my breath smelling of brimstone, I really can't help it, and I once met a man whose breath smelled of onions, which I consider far worse."

"I don't," said Betsy; "I love onions."

"And I love brimstone," declared the dragon, "so don't let us quarrel over one another's peculiarities."

Saying this, he breathed a long breath and shot a flame fifty feet from his mouth. The brimstone made Betsy cough, but she remembered about the onions and said nothing.

They had no idea how far they had gone through the center of the earth, nor when to expect the trip to end. At one time the little girl remarked:

"I wonder when we'll reach the bottom of this hole. And isn't it funny, Shaggy Man, that what is the bottom to us now, was the top when we fell the other way?"

"What puzzles me," said Files, "is that we are able to fall both ways."

"That," announced Tik-Tok, "is be-cause the world is round."

"Exactly," responded Shaggy. "The machinery in your head is in fine working order, Tik-Tok. You know, Betsy, that there is such a thing as the Attraction of Gravitation, which draws everything toward the center of the earth. That is why we fall out of bed, and why everything clings to the surface of the earth."

"Then why doesn't everything go on down to the center of the earth?" inquired the little girl.

"I was afraid you were going to ask me that," replied Shaggy in a sad tone. "The reason, my dear, is that the earth is so solid that other solid things can't get through it. But when there's a hole, as there is in this case, we drop right down to the center of the world."

"Why don't we stop there?" asked Betsy.

"Because we go so fast that we acquire speed enough to carry us right up to the other end."

"I don't understand that, and it makes my head ache to try to figure it out," she said after some thought. "One thing draws us to the center and another thing pushes us away from it. But—"

"Don't ask me why, please," interrupted the Shaggy Man. "If you can't understand it, let it go at that."

"Do *you* understand it?" she inquired.

"All the magic isn't in fairyland," he said gravely. "There's lots of magic in all Nature, and you may see it as well in the United States, where you and I once lived, as you can here."

"I never did," she replied.

"Because you were so used to it all that you didn't realize it was magic. Is anything more wonderful than to see a flower grow and blossom, or to get light out of the electricity in the air? The cows that manufacture milk for us must have machinery fully as remarkable as that in Tik-Tok's copper body, and perhaps you've noticed that—"

And then, before Shaggy could finish his speech, the strong light of day suddenly broke upon them, grew brighter, and completely enveloped them. The dragon's claws no longer scraped against the metal Tube, for he shot into the open air a hundred feet or more and sailed so far away from the slanting hole that when he landed it was on the peak of a mountain and just over the entrance to the many underground caverns of the Nome King.

Some of the officers tumbled off their seats when Quox struck the ground, but most of the dragon's passengers only felt a slight jar. All were glad to be on solid earth again and they at once dismounted and began to look about them. Queerly enough, as soon as they had left the dragon, the seats that were strapped to the monster's back disappeared, and this probably happened because there was no further use for them and because Quox looked far more dignified in just his silver scales. Of course he still wore the forty yards of ribbon around his neck, as well as the great locket, but these only made him look "dressed up," as Betsy remarked.

Now the army of nomes had gathered thickly around the mouth of the Tube, in order to be ready to capture the band of invaders as soon as they popped out. There were, indeed, hundreds of nomes assembled, and they were led by Guph, their most famous General. But they did not expect the dragon to fly so high, and he shot out of the Tube so suddenly that it took them by surprise. When the nomes had rubbed the astonishment out of their eyes and regained their wits, they discovered the dragon quietly seated on the mountain-side far above their heads, while the other strangers were standing in a group and calmly looking down upon them.

General Guph was very angry at the escape, which was no one's fault but his own.

"Come down here and be captured!" he shouted, waving his sword at them.

"Come up here and capture us—if you dare!" replied Queen Ann, who was winding up the clockwork of her Private Soldier, so he could fight more briskly.

Guph's first answer was a roar of rage at the defiance; then he turned and issued a command to his nomes. These were all armed with sharp spears and with one accord they raised these spears and threw them straight at their foes, so that they rushed through the air in a perfect cloud of flying weapons.

Some damage might have been done had not the dragon quickly crawled before the others, his body being so big that

164

it shielded every one of them, including Hank. The spears rattled against the silver scales of Quox and then fell harmlessly to the ground. They were magic spears, of course, and all straightway bounded back into the hands of those who had thrown them, but even Guph could see that it was useless to repeat the attack.

It was now Queen Ann's turn to attack, so the Generals yelled "For—ward march!" and the Colonels and Majors and Captains repeated the command and the valiant Army of Oogaboo, which seemed to be composed mainly of Tik-Tok, marched forward in single column toward the nomes, while Betsy and Polychrome cheered and Hank gave a loud "Hee-haw!" and Shaggy shouted "Hooray!" and Queen Ann screamed: "At 'em, Tik-Tok—at 'em!"

The nomes did not await the Clockwork Man's attack but in a twinkling disappeared into the underground caverns. They made a great mistake in being so hasty, for Tik-Tok had not taken a dozen steps before he stubbed his copper toe on a rock and fell flat to the ground, where he cried: "Pick me up! Pick me up! Pick me up!" until Shaggy and Files ran forward and raised him to his feet again.

The dragon chuckled softly to himself as he scratched his left ear with his hind claw, but no one was paying much attention to Quox just then.

It was evident to Ann and her officers that there could be

no fighting unless the enemy was present, and in order to find the enemy they must boldly enter the underground Kingdom of the nomes. So bold a step demanded a council of war.

"Don't you think I'd better drop in on Ruggedo and obey the orders of the Jinjin?" asked Quox.

"By no means!" returned Queen Ann. "We have already put the army of nomes to flight and all that yet remains is to force our way into those caverns and conquer the Nome King and all his people."

"That seems to me something of a job," said the dragon, closing his eyes sleepily. "But go ahead, if you like, and I'll wait here for you. Don't be in any hurry on my account. To one who lives thousands of years the delay of a few days means nothing at all, and I shall probably sleep until the time comes for me to act."

Ann was provoked at this speech.

"You may as well go back to Tititi-Hoochoo now," she said, "for the Nome King is as good as conquered already."

But Quox shook his head. "No," said he; "I'll wait."

CHAPTER 16

The Naughty Nome

SHAGGY MAN had said nothing during the conversation between Queen Ann and Quox, for the simple reason that he did not consider the matter worth an argument. Safe within his pocket reposed the Love Magnet, which had never failed to win every heart. The nomes, he knew, were not like the heartless Roses and therefore could be won to his side as soon as he exhibited the magic talisman.

Shaggy's chief anxiety had been to reach Ruggedo's Kingdom and now that the entrance lay before him he was confident he would be able to rescue his lost brother. Let Ann and the dragon quarrel as to who should conquer the nomes, if they liked; Shaggy would let them try, and if they failed he had the means of conquest in his own pocket.

But Ann was positive she could not fail, for she thought her Army could do anything. So she called the officers together and told them how to act, and she also instructed Tik-Tok what to do and what to say.

"Please do not shoot your gun except as a last resort," she added, "for I do not wish to be cruel or to shed any blood— unless it is absolutely necessary."

"All right," replied Tik-Tok; "but I do not think Rug-ge-do would bleed if I filled him full of holes and put him in a ci-der press."

Then the officers fell in line, the four Generals abreast and then the four Colonels and the four Majors and the four Captains. They drew their glittering swords and com-manded Tik-Tok to march, which he did. Twice he fell down, being tripped by the rough rocks, but when he struck the smooth path he got along better. Into the gloomy mouth of the cavern entrance he stepped without hesitation, and after him proudly pranced the officers and Queen Ann. The others held back a little, waiting to see what would happen.

Of course the Nome King knew they were coming and was prepared to receive them. Just within the rocky passage that led to the jeweled throne-room was a deep pit, which was usually covered. Ruggedo had ordered the cover removed and it now stood open, scarcely visible in the gloom.

Tik-Tok of Oz

The pit was so large around that it nearly filled the passage and there was barely room for one to walk around it by pressing close to the rock walls. This Tik-Tok did, for his copper eyes saw the pit clearly and he avoided it; but the officers marched straight into the hole and tumbled in a heap on the bottom. An instant later Queen Ann also walked into the pit, for she had her chin in the air and was careless where she placed her feet. Then one of the nomes pulled a lever which replaced the cover on the pit and made the officers of Oogaboo and their Queen fast prisoners.

As for Tik-Tok, he kept straight on to the cavern where Ruggedo sat in his throne and there he faced the Nome King and said:

"I here-by con-quer you in the name of Queen Ann So-forth of Oo-ga-boo, whose Ar-my I am, and I de-clare that you are her pris-on-er!"

Ruggedo laughed at him.

"Where is this famous Queen?" he asked.

"She'll be here in a min-ute," said Tik-Tok. "Per-haps she stopped to tie her shoe-string."

"Now, see here, Tik-Tok," began the Nome King, in a stern voice, "I've had enough of this nonsense. Your Queen and her officers are all prisoners, having fallen into my power, so perhaps you'll tell me what you mean to do."

"My or-ders were to con-quer you," replied Tik-Tok,

"and my ma-chin-er-y has done the best it knows how to car-ry out those or-ders."

Ruggedo pounded on his gong and Kaliko appeared, followed closely by General Guph.

"Take this copper man into the shops and set him to work hammering gold," commanded the King. "Being run by machinery he ought to be a steady worker. He ought never to have been made, but since he exists I shall hereafter put him to good use."

"If you try to cap-ture me," said Tik-Tok, "I shall fight."

"Don't do that!" exclaimed General Guph, earnestly, "for it will be useless to resist and you might hurt some one."

But Tik-Tok raised his gun and took aim and not knowing what damage the gun might do the nomes were afraid to face it.

While he was thus defying the Nome King and his high officials, Betsy Bobbin rode calmly into the royal cavern, seated upon the back of Hank the mule. The little girl had grown tired of waiting for "something to happen" and so had come to see if Ruggedo had been conquered.

"Nails and nuggets!" roared the King; "how dare you bring that beast here and enter my presence unannounced?"

"There wasn't anybody to announce me," replied Betsy. "I guess your folks were all busy. Are you conquered yet?"

"No!" shouted the King, almost beside himself with rage.

Chapter Sixteen

"Then please give me something to eat, for I'm awful hungry," said the girl. "You see, this conquering business is a good deal like waiting for a circus parade; it takes a long time to get around and don't amount to much anyhow."

The nomes were so much astonished at this speech that for a time they could only glare at her silently, not finding words to reply. The King finally recovered the use of his tongue and said:

"Earth-crawler! this insolence to my majesty shall be your death-warrant. You are an ordinary mortal, and to stop a mortal from living is so easy a thing to do that I will not keep you waiting half so long as you did for my conquest."

"I'd rather you wouldn't stop me from living," remarked Betsy, getting off Hank's back and standing beside him. "And it would be a pretty cheap King who killed a visitor while she was hungry. If you'll give me something to eat, I'll talk this killing business over with you afterward; only, I warn you now that I don't approve of it, and never will."

Her coolness and lack of fear impressed the Nome King, although he bore an intense hatred toward all mortals.

"What do you wish to eat?" he asked gruffly.

"Oh, a ham-sandwich would do, or perhaps a couple of hard-boiled eggs—"

"Eggs!" shrieked the three nomes who were present, shuddering till their teeth chattered.

"What's the matter?" asked Betsy wonderingly. "Are eggs as high here as they are at home?"

"Guph," said the King in an agitated voice, turning to his General, "let us destroy this rash mortal at once! Seize her and take her to the Slimy Cave and lock her in."

Guph glanced at Tik-Tok, whose gun was still pointed, but just then Kaliko stole softly behind the copper man and kicked his knee-joints so that they suddenly bent forward and tumbled Tik-Tok to the floor, his gun falling from his grasp.

Then Guph, seeing Tik-Tok helpless, made a grab at Betsy. At the same time Hank's heels shot out and caught the General just where his belt was buckled. He rose into the air swift as a cannon-ball, struck the Nome King fairly and flattened his Majesty against the wall of rock on the opposite side of the cavern. Together they fell to the floor in a dazed and crumpled condition, seeing which Kaliko whispered to Betsy:

"Come with me—quick!—and I will save you."

She looked into Kaliko's face inquiringly and thought he seemed honest and good-natured, so she decided to follow him. He led her and the mule through several passages and into a small cavern very nicely and comfortably furnished.

"This is my own room," said he, "but you are quite welcome to use it. Wait here a minute and I'll get you something to eat."

Chapter Sixteen

When Kaliko returned he brought a tray containing some broiled mushrooms, a loaf of mineral bread and some petroleum-butter. The butter Betsy could not eat, but the bread was good and the mushrooms delicious.

"Here's the door key," said Kaliko, "and you'd better lock yourself in."

"Won't you let Polychrome and the Rose Princess come here, too?" she asked.

"I'll see. Where are they?"

"I don't know. I left them outside," said Betsy.

"Well, if you hear three raps on the door, open it," said Kaliko; "but don't let anyone in unless they give the three raps."

"All right," promised Betsy, and when Kaliko left the cosy cavern she closed and locked the door.

In the meantime Ann and her officers, finding themselves prisoners in the pit, had shouted and screamed until they were tired out, but no one had come to their assistance. It was very dark and damp in the pit and they could not climb out because the walls were higher than their heads and the cover was on. The Queen was first angry and then annoyed and then discouraged; but the officers were only afraid. Every one of the poor fellows heartily wished he was back in Oogaboo caring for his orchard, and some were so unhappy that they began to reproach Ann for causing them all this trouble and danger.

Finally the Queen sat down on the bottom of the pit and leaned her back against the wall. By good luck her sharp elbow touched a secret spring in the wall and a big flat rock swung inward. Ann fell over backward, but the next instant she jumped up and cried to the others:

"A passage! A passage! Follow me, my brave men, and we may yet escape."

Then she began to crawl through the passage, which was as dark and dank as the pit, and the officers followed her in single file. They crawled, and they crawled, and they kept on crawling, for the passage was not big enough to allow them to stand upright. It turned this way and twisted that, sometimes like a corkscrew and sometimes zigzag, but seldom ran for long in a straight line.

"It will never end—never!" moaned the officers, who were rubbing all the skin off their knees on the rough rooks.

"It *must* end," retorted Ann courageously, "or it never would have been made. We don't know where it will lead us to, but any place is better than that loathsome pit."

So she crawled on, and the officers crawled on, and while they were crawling through this awful underground passage Polychrome and Shaggy and Files and the Rose Princess, who were standing outside the entrance to Ruggedo's domains, were wondering what had become of them.

CHAPTER 17

A Tragic Transformation

"DON'T let us worry," said Shaggy to his companions, "for it may take the Queen some time to conquer the Metal Monarch, as Tik-Tok has to do everything in his slow, mechanical way."

"Do you suppose they are likely to fail?" asked the Rose Princess.

"I do, indeed," replied Shaggy. "This Nome King is really a powerful fellow and has a legion of nomes to assist him, whereas our bold Queen commands a Clockwork Man and a band of faint-hearted officers."

"She ought to have let Quox do the conquering," said Polychrome, dancing lightly upon a point of rock and fluttering her beautiful draperies. "But perhaps the dragon was wise to let her go first, for when she fails to conquer Ruggedo she may become more modest in her ambitions."

"Where is the dragon now?" inquired Ozga.

"Up there on the rocks," replied Files. "Look, my dear; you may see him from here. He said he would take a little nap while we were mixing up with Ruggedo, and he added that after we had gotten into trouble he would wake up and conquer the Nome King in a jiffy, as his master the Jinjin has ordered him to do."

"Quox means well," said Shaggy, "but I do not think we shall need his services; for just as soon as I am satisfied that Queen Ann and her army have failed to conquer Ruggedo. I shall enter the caverns and show the King my Love Magnet. That he cannot resist; therefore the conquest will be made with ease."

This speech of Shaggy Man's was overheard by the Long-Eared Hearer, who was at that moment standing by Ruggedo's side. For when the King and Guph had recovered from Hank's kick and had picked themselves up, their first act was to turn Tik-Tok on his back and put a heavy diamond on top of him, so that he could not get up again. Then they carefully put his gun in a corner of the cavern and the King sent Guph to fetch the Long-Eared Hearer.

The Hearer was still angry at Ruggedo for breaking his

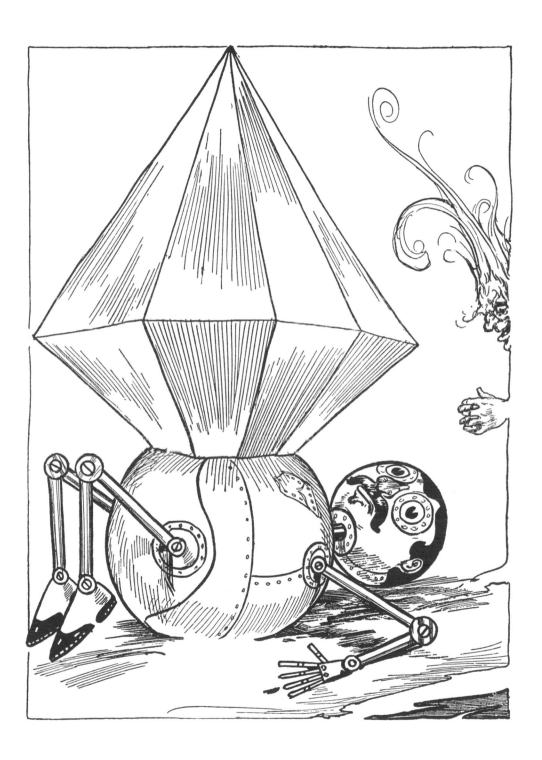

ear, but he acknowledged the Nome King to be his master and was ready to obey his commands. Therefore he repeated Shaggy's speech to the King, who at once realized that his Kingdom was in grave danger. For Ruggedo knew of the Love Magnet and its powers and was horrified at the thought that Shaggy might show him the magic talisman and turn all the hatred in his heart into love. Ruggedo was proud of his hatred and abhorred love of any sort.

"Really," said he, "I'd rather be conquered and lose my wealth and my Kingdom than gaze at that awful Love Magnet. What can I do to prevent the Shaggy Man from taking it out of his pocket?"

Kaliko returned to the cavern in time to overhear this question, and being a loyal nome and eager to serve his King, he answered by saying:

"If we can manage to bind the Shaggy Man's arms, tight to his body, he could not get the Love Magnet out of his pocket.

"True!" cried the King in delight at this easy solution of the problem. "Get at once a dozen nomes, with ropes, and place them in the passage where they can seize and bind Shaggy as soon as he enters."

This Kaliko did, and meanwhile the watchers outside the entrance were growing more and more uneasy about their friends.

"I don't worry so much about the Oogaboo people," said Polychrome, who had grown sober with waiting, and perhaps a little nervous, "for they could not be killed, even though Ruggedo might cause them much suffering and perhaps destroy them utterly. But we should not have allowed Betsy and Hank to go alone into the caverns. The little girl is mortal and possesses no magic powers whatever, so if Ruggedo captures her she will be wholly at his mercy."

"That is indeed true," replied Shaggy. "I wouldn't like to have anything happen to dear little Betsy, so I believe I'll go in right away and put an end to all this worry."

"We may as well go with you," asserted Files, "for by means of the Love Magnet you can soon bring the Nome King to reason."

So it was decided to wait no longer. Shaggy walked through the entrance first, and after him came the others. They had no thought of danger to themselves, and Shaggy, who was going along with his hands thrust into his pockets, was much surprised when a rope shot out from the darkness and twined around his body, pinning down his arms so securely that he could not even withdraw his hands from the pockets. Then appeared several grinning nomes, who speedily tied knots in the ropes and then led the prisoner along the passage to the cavern. No attention was paid to the others, but Files and the Princess followed on after

Shaggy, determined not to desert their friend and hoping that an opportunity might arise to rescue him.

As for Polychrome, as soon as she saw that trouble had overtaken Shaggy she turned and ran lightly back through the passage and out of the entrance. Then she easily leaped from rock to rock until she paused beside the great dragon, who lay fast asleep.

"Wake up, Quox!" she cried. "It is time for you to act."

But Quox did not wake up. He lay as one in a trance, absolutely motionless, with his enormous eyes tight closed. The eyelids had big silver scales on them, like all the rest of his body.

Polychrome might have thought Quox was dead had she not known that dragons do not die easily or had she not observed his huge body swelling as he breathed. She picked up a piece of rock and pounded against his eyelids with it, saying:

"Wake up, Quox—wake up!" But he would not waken.

"Dear me, how unfortunate!" sighed the lovely Rainbow's Daughter. "I wonder what is the best and surest way to waken a dragon. All our friends may be captured and destroyed while this great beast lies asleep."

She walked around Quox two or three times, trying to discover some tender place on his body where a thump or a punch might be felt; but he lay extended along the rocks

with his chin flat upon the ground and his legs drawn underneath his body, and all that one could see was his thick sky-blue skin—thicker than that of a rhinoceros—and his silver scales.

Then, despairing at last of wakening the beast, and worried over the fate of her friends, Polychrome again ran down to the entrance and hurried along the passage into the Nome King's cavern.

Here she found Ruggedo lolling in his throne and smoking a long pipe. Beside him stood General Guph and Kaliko, and ranged before the King were the Rose Princess, Files and the Shaggy Man. Tik-Tok still lay upon the floor, weighted down by the big diamond.

Ruggedo was now in a more contented frame of mind. One by one he had met the invaders and easily captured them. The dreaded Love Magnet was indeed in Shaggy's pocket, only a few feet away from the King, but Shaggy was powerless to show it and unless Ruggedo's eyes beheld the talisman it could not affect him. As for Betsy Bobbin and her mule, he believed Kaliko had placed them in the Slimy Cave, while Ann and her officers he thought safely imprisoned in the pit. Ruggedo had no fear of Files or Ozga, but to be on the safe side he had ordered golden handcuffs placed upon their wrists. These did not cause them any great annoyance but prevented them from making an attack, had they been inclined to do so.

Chapter Seventeen

The Nome King, thinking himself wholly master of the situation, was laughing and jeering at his prisoners when Polychrome, exquisitely beautiful and dancing like a ray of light, entered the cavern.

"Oho!" cried the King; "a Rainbow under ground, eh?" and then he stared hard at Polychrome, and still harder, and then he sat up and pulled the wrinkles out of his robe and arranged his whiskers. "On my word," said he, "you are a very captivating creature; moreover, I perceive you are a fairy."

"I am Polychrome, the Rainbow's Daughter," she said proudly.

"Well," replied Ruggedo, "I like you. The others I hate. I hate everybody—but you! Wouldn't you like to live always in this beautiful cavern, Polychrome? See! the jewels that stud the walls have every tint and color of your Rainbow—and they are not so elusive. I'll have fresh dewdrops gathered for your feasting every day and you shall be Queen of all my nomes and pull Kaliko's nose whenever you like."

"No, thank you," laughed Polychrome. "My home is in the sky, and I'm only on a visit to this solid, sordid earth. But tell me, Ruggedo, why my friends have been wound with cords and bound with chains?"

"They threatened me," answered Ruggedo. "The fools did not know how powerful I am."

"Then, since they are now helpless, why not release them and send them back to the earth's surface?"

"Because I hate 'em and mean to make 'em suffer for their invasion. But I'll make a bargain with you, sweet Polly. Remain here and live with me and I'll set all these people free. You shall be my daughter or my wife or my aunt or grandmother—whichever you like—only stay here to brighten my gloomy kingdom and make me happy!"

Polychrome looked at him wonderingly. Then she turned to Shaggy and asked:

"Are you sure he hasn't seen the Love Magnet?"

"I'm positive," answered Shaggy. "But you seem to be something of a Love Magnet yourself, Polychrome."

She laughed again and said to Ruggedo: "Not even to rescue my friends would I live in your kingdom. Nor could I endure for long the society of such a wicked monster as you."

"You forget," retorted the King, scowling darkly, "that you also are in my power."

"Not so, Ruggedo. The Rainbow's Daughter is beyond the reach of your spite or malice."

"Seize her!" suddenly shouted the King, and General Guph sprang forward to obey. Polychrome stood quite still, yet when Guph attempted to clutch her his hands met in air, and now the Rainbow's Daughter was in another part of the room, as smiling and composed as before.

Several times Guph endeavored to capture her and Ruggedo even came down from his throne to assist his General; but never could they lay hands upon the lovely sky fairy, who flitted here and there with the swiftness of light and constantly defied them with her merry laughter as she evaded their efforts.

So after a time they abandoned the chase and Ruggedo returned to his throne and wiped the perspiration from his face with a finely-woven handkerchief of cloth-of-gold.

"Well," said Polychrome, "what do you intend to do now?"

"I'm going to have some fun, to repay me for all my bother," replied the Nome King. Then he said to Kaliko: "Summon the executioners."

Kaliko at once withdrew and presently returned with a score of nomes, all of whom were nearly as evil looking as their hated master. They bore great golden pincers, and prods of silver, and clamps and chains and various wicked-looking instruments, all made of precious metals and set with diamonds and rubies.

"Now, Pang," said Ruggedo, addressing the leader of the executioners, "fetch the Army of Oogaboo and their Queen from the pit and torture them here in my presence—as well as in the presence of their friends. It will be great sport."

"I hear Your Majesty, and I obey Your Majesty,"

answered Pang, and went with his nomes into the passage. In a few minutes he returned and bowed to Ruggedo.

"They're all gone," said he.

"Gone!" exclaimed the Nome King. "Gone where?"

"They left no address, Your Majesty; but they are not in the pit."

"Picks and puddles!" roared the King; "who took the cover off?"

"No one," said Pang. "The cover was there, but the prisoners were not under it."

"In that case," snarled the King, trying to control his disappointment, "go to the Slimy Cave and fetch hither the girl and the donkey. And while we are torturing them Kaliko must take a hundred nomes and search for the escaped prisoners—the Queen of Oogaboo and her officers. If he does not find them, I will torture Kaliko."

Kaliko went away looking sad and disturbed, for he knew the King was cruel and unjust enough to carry out this threat. Pang and the executioners also went away, in another direction, but when they came back Betsy Bobbin was not with them, nor was Hank.

"There is no one in the Slimy Cave, Your Majesty," reported Pang.

"Jumping jellycakes!" screamed the King. "Another escape? Are you sure you found the right cave?"

"There is but one Slimy Cave, and there is no one in it," returned Pang positively.

Ruggedo was beginning to be alarmed as well as angry. However, these disappointments but made him the more vindictive and he cast an evil look at the other prisoners and said:

"Never mind the girl and the donkey. Here are four, at least, who cannot escape my vengeance. Let me see; I believe I'll change my mind about Tik-Tok. Have the gold crucible heated to a white, seething heat, and then we'll dump the copper man into it and melt him up."

"But, Your Majesty," protested Kaliko, who had returned to the room after sending a hundred nomes to search for the Oogaboo people, "you must remember that Tik-Tok is a very curious and interesting machine. It would be a shame to deprive the world of such a clever contrivance."

"Say another word, and you'll go into the furnace with him!" roared the King. "I'm getting tired of you, Kaliko, and the first thing you know I'll turn you into a potato and make Saratoga-chips of you! The next to consider," he added more mildly, "is the Shaggy Man. As he owns the Love Magnet, I think I'll transform him into a dove, and then we can practice shooting at him with Tik-Tok's gun. Now, this is a very interesting ceremony and I beg you all to watch me closely and see that I've nothing up my sleeve."

He came out of his throne to stand before the Shaggy

Chapter Seventeen

Man, and then he waved his hands, palms downward, in seven semicircles over his victim's head, saying in a low but clear tone of voice the magic wugwa:

"Adi, edi, idi, odi, udi, oo-i-oo!
Idu, ido, idi, ide, ida, woo!"

The effect of this well-known sorcery was instantaneous. Instead of the Shaggy Man, a pretty dove lay fluttering upon the floor, its wings confined by tiny cords wound around them. Ruggedo gave an order to Pang, who cut the cords with a pair of scissors. Being freed, the dove quickly flew upward and alighted on the shoulder of the Rose Princess, who stroked it tenderly.

"Very good! Very good!" cried Ruggedo, rubbing his hands gleefully together. "One enemy is out of my way, and now for the others."

(Perhaps my readers should be warned not to attempt the above transformation; for, although the exact magical formula has been described, it is unlawful in all civilized countries for anyone to transform a person into a dove by muttering the words Ruggedo used. There were no laws to prevent the Nome King from performing this transformation, but if it should be attempted in any other country, and the magic worked, the magician would be severely punished.)

When Polychrome saw Shaggy Man transformed into a dove and realized that Ruggedo was about to do something as dreadful to the Princess and Files, and that Tik-Tok would soon be melted in a crucible, she turned and ran from the cavern, through the passage and back to the place where Quox lay asleep.

CHAPTER 18

A Clever Conquest

THE great dragon still had his eyes closed and was even snoring in a manner that resembled distant thunder; but Polychrome was now desperate, because any further delay meant the destruction of her friends. She seized the pearl necklace, to which was attached the great locket, and jerked it with all her strength.

The result was encouraging. Quox stopped snoring and his eyelids flickered. So Polychrome jerked again—and again—till slowly the great lids raised and the dragon looked at her steadily. Said he, in a sleepy tone:

"What's the matter, little Rainbow?"

"Come quick!" exclaimed Polychrome. "Ruggedo has captured all our friends and is about to destroy them."

"Well, well," said Quox, "I suspected that would happen. Step a little out of my path, my dear, and I'll make a rush for the Nome King's cavern."

She fell back a few steps and Quox raised himself on his stout legs, whisked his long tail and in an instant had slid down the rocks and made a dive through the entrance.

Along the passage he swept, nearly filling it with his immense body, and now he poked his head into the jeweled cavern of Ruggedo.

But the King had long since made arrangements to capture the dragon, whenever he might appear. No sooner did Quox stick his head into the room than a thick chain fell from above and encircled his neck. Then the ends of the chain were drawn tight—for in an adjoining cavern a thousand nomes were pulling on them—and so the dragon could advance no further toward the King. He could not use his teeth or his claws and as his body was still in the passage he had not even room to strike his foes with his terrible tail.

Ruggedo was delighted with the success of his strategem. He had just transformed the Rose Princess into a fiddle and was about to transform Files into a fiddle bow, when the dragon appeared to interrupt him. So he called out:

"Welcome, my dear Quox, to my royal entertainment. Since you are here, you shall witness some very neat magic,

Chapter Eighteen

and after I have finished with Files and Tik-Tok I mean to transform you into a tiny lizard—one of the chameleon sort—and you shall live in my cavern and amuse me."

"Pardon me for contradicting Your Majesty," returned Quox in a quiet voice, "but I don't believe you'll perform any more magic."

"Eh? Why not?" asked the King in surprise.

"There's a reason," said Quox. "Do you see this ribbon around my neck?"

"Yes; and I'm astonished that a dignified dragon should wear such a silly thing."

"Do you see it plainly?" persisted the dragon, with a little chuckle of amusement.

"I do," declared Ruggedo.

"Then you no longer possess any magical powers, and are as helpless as a clam," asserted Quox. "My great master, Tititi-Hoochoo, the Jinjin, enchanted this ribbon in such a way that whenever Your Majesty looked upon it all knowledge of magic would desert you instantly, nor will any magical formula you can remember ever perform your bidding."

"Pooh! I don't believe a word of it!" cried Ruggedo, half frightened, nevertheless. Then he turned toward Files and tried to transform him into a fiddle bow. But he could not remember the right words or the right pass of the hands and after several trials he finally gave up the attempt.

Tik-Tok of Oz

By this time the Nome King was so alarmed that he was secretly shaking in his shoes.

"I told you not to anger Tititi-Hoochoo," grumbled Kaliko, "and now you see the result of your disobedience."

Ruggedo promptly threw his sceptre at his Royal Chamberlain, who dodged it with his usual cleverness, and then he said with an attempt to swagger:

"Never mind; I don't need magic to enable me to destroy these invaders; fire and the sword will do the business and I am still King of the Nomes and lord and master of my Underground Kingdom!"

"Again I beg to differ with Your Majesty," said Quox. "The Great Jinjin commands you to depart instantly from this Kingdom and seek the earth's surface, where you will wander for all time to come, without a home or country, without a friend or follower, and without any more riches than you can carry with you in your pockets. The Great Jinjin is so generous that he will allow you to fill your pockets with jewels or gold, but you must take nothing more."

Ruggedo now stared at the dragon in amazement.

"Does Tititi-Hoochoo condemn me to such a fate?" he asked in a hoarse voice.

"He does," said Quox.

"And just for throwing a few strangers down the Forbidden Tube?"

Chapter Eighteen

"Just for that," repeated Quox in a stern, gruff voice.

"Well, I won't do it. And your crazy old Jinjin can't make me do it, either!" declared Ruggedo. "I intend to remain here, King of the Nomes, until the end of the world, and I defy your Tititi-Hoochoo and all his fairies—as well as his clumsy messenger, whom I have been obliged to chain up!"

The dragon smiled again, but it was not the sort of smile that made Ruggedo feel very happy. Instead, there was something so cold and merciless in the dragon's expression that the condemned Nome King trembled and was sick at heart.

There was little comfort for Ruggedo in the fact that the dragon was now chained, although he had boasted of it. He glared at the immense head of Quox as if fascinated and there was fear in the old King's eyes as he watched his enemy's movements.

For the dragon was now moving; not abruptly, but as if he had something to do and was about to do it. Very deliberately he raised one claw, touched the catch of the great jeweled locket that was suspended around his neck, and at once it opened wide.

Nothing much happened at first; half a dozen hen's eggs rolled out upon the floor and then the locket closed with a sharp click. But the effect upon the nomes of this simple thing was astounding. General Guph, Kaliko, Pang and his band of executioners were all standing close to the door that led to the vast series of underground caverns which constituted the dominions of the nomes, and as soon as they saw the eggs they raised a chorus of frantic screams and rushed through the door, slamming it in Ruggedo's face and placing a heavy bronze bar across it.

Ruggedo, dancing with terror and uttering loud cries, now leaped upon the seat of his throne to escape the eggs, which had rolled steadily toward him. Perhaps these eggs, sent by the wise and crafty Tititi-Hoochoo, were in some way enchanted, for they all rolled directly after Ruggedo and when they reached the throne where he had taken refuge they began rolling up the legs to the seat.

This was too much for the King to bear. His horror of eggs was real and absolute and he made a leap from the throne to the center of the room and then ran to a far corner.

The eggs followed, rolling slowly but steadily in his direction. Ruggedo threw his sceptre at them, and then his ruby crown, and then he drew off his heavy golden sandals and hurled these at the advancing eggs. But the eggs dodged every missile and continued to draw nearer. The King stood trembling, his eyes staring in terror, until they were but half a yard distant; then with an agile leap he jumped clear over them and made a rush for the passage that led to the outer entrance.

Of course the dragon was in his way, being chained in the

Chapter Eighteen

passage with his head in the cavern, but when he saw the King making toward him he crouched as low as he could and dropped his chin to the floor, leaving a small space between his body and the roof of the passage.

Ruggedo did not hesitate an instant. Impelled by fear, he leaped to the dragon's nose and then scrambled to his back, where he succeeded in squeezing himself through the opening. After the head was passed there was more room and he slid along the dragon's scales to his tail and then ran as fast as his legs would carry him to the entrance. Not pausing here, so great was his fright, the King dashed on down the mountain path, but before he had gone very far he stumbled and fell.

When he picked himself up he observed that no one was following him, and while he recovered his breath he happened to think of the decree of the Jinjin—that he should be driven from his Kingdom and made a wanderer on the face of the earth. Well, here he was, driven from his cavern in truth; driven by those dreadful eggs; but he would go back and defy them; he would not submit to losing his precious Kingdom and his tyrannical powers, all because Tititi-Hoochoo had said he must.

So, although still afraid, Ruggedo nerved himself to creep back along the path to the entrance, and when he arrived there he saw the six eggs lying in a row just before the arched opening.

At first he paused a safe distance away to consider the case, for the eggs were now motionless. While he was wondering what could be done, he remembered there was a magical charm which would destroy eggs and render them harmless to nomes. There were nine passes to be made and six verses of incantation to be recited; but Ruggedo knew them all. Now that he had ample time to be exact, he carefully went through the entire ceremony.

But nothing happened. The eggs did not disappear, as he had expected; so he repeated the charm a second time. When that also failed, he remembered, with a moan of despair, that his magic power had been taken away from him and in the future he could do no more than any common mortal.

And there were the eggs, forever barring him from the Kingdom which he had ruled so long with absolute sway! He threw rocks at them, but could not hit a single egg. He raved and scolded and tore his hair and beard, and danced in helpless passion, but that did nothing to avert the just judgment of the Jinjin, which Ruggedo's own evil deeds had brought upon him.

From this time on he was an outcast—a wanderer upon the face of the earth—and he had even forgotten to fill his pockets with gold and jewels before he fled from his former Kingdom!

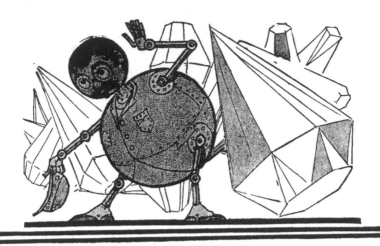

CHAPTER 19

King Kaliko

AFTER the King had made good his escape Files said to the dragon, in a said voice:

"Alas! why did you not come before? Because you were sleeping instead of conquering, the lovely Rose Princess has become a fiddle without a bow, while poor Shaggy sits there a cooing dove!"

"Don't worry," replied Quox. "Tititi-Hoochoo knows his business, and I had my orders from the Great Jinjin himself. Bring the fiddle here and touch it lightly to my pink ribbon."

Files obeyed and at the moment of contact with the ribbon the Nome King's charm was broken and the Rose Princess herself stood before them as sweet and smiling as ever.

The dove, perched on the back of the throne, had seen and heard all this, so without being told what to do it flew straight to the dragon and alighted on the ribbon. Next instant Shaggy was himself again and Quox said to him grumblingly:

"Please get off any left toe, Shaggy Man, and be more particular where you step."

"I beg your pardon!" replied Shaggy, very glad to resume his natural form. Then he ran to lift the heavy diamond off Tik-Tok's chest and to assist the Clockwork Man to his feet.

"Ma-ny thanks!" said Tik-Tok. "Where is the wick-ed King who want-ed to melt me in a cru-ci-ble?"

"He has gone, and gone for good," answered Polychrome, who had managed to squeeze into the room beside the dragon and had witnessed the occurrences with much interest. "But I wonder where Betsy Bobbin and Hank can be, and if any harm has befallen them."

"We must search the cavern until we find them," declared Shaggy; but when he went to the door leading to the other caverns he found it shut and barred.

"I've a pretty strong push in my forehead," said Quox, "and I believe I can break down that door, even though it's made of solid gold."

"But you are a prisoner, and the chains that hold you are

fastened in some other room, so that we cannot release you," Files said anxiously.

"Oh, never mind that," returned the dragon. "I have remained a prisoner only because I wished to be one," and with this he stepped forward and burst the stout chains as easily as if they had been threads.

But when he tried to push in the heavy metal door, even his mighty strength failed, and after several attempts he gave it up and squatted himself in a corner to think of a better way.

"I'll o-pen the door," asserted Tik-Tok, and going to the King's big gong he pounded upon it until the noise was almost deafening.

Kaliko, in the next cavern, was wondering what had happened to Ruggedo and if he had escaped the eggs and outwitted the dragon. But when he heard the sound of the gong, which had so often called him into the King's presence, he decided that Ruggedo had been victorious; so he took away the bar, threw open the door and entered the royal cavern.

Great was his astonishment to find the King gone and the enchantments removed from the Princess and Shaggy. But the eggs were also gone and so Kaliko advanced to the dragon, whom he knew to be Tititi-Hoochoo's messenger, and bowed humbly before the beast.

"What is your will?" he inquired.

"Where is Betsy?" demanded the dragon.

"Safe in my own private room," said Kaliko.

"Go and get her!" commanded Quox.

So Kaliko went to Betsy's room and gave three raps upon the door. The little girl had been asleep, but she heard the raps and opened the door.

"You may come out now," said Kaliko. "The King has fled in disgrace and your friends are asking for you."

So Betsy and Hank returned with the Royal Chamberlain to the throne cavern, where she was received with great joy by her friends. They told her what had happened to Ruggedo and she told them how kind Kaliko had been to her. Quox did not have much to say until the conversation was ended, but then he turned to Kaliko and asked:

"Do you suppose you could rule your nomes better than Ruggedo has done?"

"Me?" stammered the Chamberlain, greatly surprised by the question. "Well, I couldn't be a worse King, I'm sure."

"Would the nomes obey you?" inquired the dragon.

"Of course," said Kaliko. "They like me better than ever they did Ruggedo."

"Then hereafter you shall be the Metal Monarch, King of the Nomes, and Tititi-Hoochoo expects you to rule your Kingdom wisely and well," said Quox.

"Hooray!" cried Betsy; "I'm glad of that. King Kaliko,

Chapter Nineteen

I salute Your Majesty and wish you joy in your gloomy old Kingdom!"

"We all wish him joy," said Polychrome; and then the others made haste to congratulate the new King.

"Will you release my dear brother?" asked Shaggy.

"The Ugly One? Very willingly," replied Kaliko. "I begged Ruggedo long ago to send him away, but he would not do so. I also offered to help your brother to escape, but he would not go."

"He's so conscientious!" said Shaggy, highly pleased. "All of our family have noble natures. But is my dear brother well?" he added anxiously.

"He eats and sleeps very steadily," replied the new King.

"I hope he doesn't work too hard," said Shaggy.

"He doesn't work at all. In fact, there is nothing he can do in these dominions as well as our nomes, whose numbers are so great that it worries us to keep them all busy. So your brother has only to amuse himself."

"Why, it's more like visiting, than being a prisoner," asserted Betsy.

"Not exactly," returned Kaliko. "A prisoner cannot go where or when he pleases, and is not his own master."

"Where is my brother now?" inquired Shaggy.

"In the Metal Forest."

"Where is that?"

"The Metal Forest is in the Great Domed Cavern, the largest in all our dominions," replied Kaliko. "It is almost like being out of doors, it is so big, and Ruggedo made the wonderful forest to amuse himself, as well as to tire out his hard-working nomes. All the trees are gold and silver and the ground is strewn with precious stones, so it is a sort of treasury."

"Let us go there at once and rescue my dear brother," pleaded Shaggy earnestly.

Kaliko hesitated.

"I don't believe I can find the way," said he. "Ruggedo made three secret passages to the Metal Forest, but he changes the location of these passages every week, so that no one can get to the Metal Forest without his permission. However, if we look sharp, we may be able to discover one of these secret ways."

"That reminds me to ask what has become of Queen Ann and the Officers of Oogaboo," said Files.

"I'm sure I can't say," replied Kaliko.

"Do you suppose Ruggedo destroyed them?"

"Oh, no; I'm quite sure he didn't. They fell into the big pit in the passage, and we put the cover on to keep them there; but when the executioners went to look for them they had all disappeared from the pit and we could find no trace of them."

Chapter Nineteen

"That's funny," remarked Betsy thoughtfully. "I don't believe Ann knew any magic, or she'd have worked it before. But to disappear like that *seems* like magic; now, doesn't it?"

They agreed that it did, but no one could explain the mystery.

"However," said Shaggy, "they are gone, that is certain, so we cannot help them or be helped by them. And the important thing just now is to rescue my dear brother from captivity."

"Why do they call him the Ugly One?" asked Betsy.

"I do not know," confessed Shaggy. "I cannot remember his looks very well, it is so long since I have seen him; but all of our family are noted for their handsome faces."

Betsy laughed and Shaggy seemed rather hurt; but Polychrome relieved his embarrassment by saying softly: "One can be ugly in looks, but lovely in disposition."

"Our first task," said Shaggy, a little comforted by this remark, "is to find one of those secret passages to the Metal Forest."

"True," agreed Kaliko. "So I think I will assemble the chief nomes of my kingdom in this throne room and tell them that I am their new King. Then I can ask them to assist us in searching for the secret passages."

"That's a good idea," said the dragon, who seemed to be getting sleepy again.

Kaliko went to the big gong and pounded on it just as Ruggedo used to do; but no one answered the summons.

"Of course not," said he, jumping up from the throne, where he had seated himself. "That is my call, and I am still the Royal Chamberlain, and will be until I appoint another in my place."

So he ran out of the room and found Guph and told him to answer the summons of the King's gong. Having returned to the royal cavern, Kaliko first pounded the gong and then sat in the throne, wearing Ruggedo's discarded ruby crown and holding in his hand the sceptre which Ruggedo had so often thrown at his head.

When Guph entered he was amazed.

"Better get out of that throne before old Ruggedo comes back," he said warningly.

"He isn't coming back, and I am now the King of the Nomes, in his stead," announced Kaliko.

"All of which is quite true," asserted the dragon, and all of those who stood around the throne bowed respectfully to the new King.

Seeing this, Guph also bowed, for he was glad to be rid of such a hard master as Ruggedo. Then Kaliko, in quite a kingly way, informed Guph that he was appointed the Royal Chamberlain, and promised not to throw the sceptre at his head unless he deserved it.

All this being pleasantly arranged, the new Chamberlain went away to tell the news to all the nomes of the underground Kingdom, every one of whom would be delighted with the change in Kings.

CHAPTER 20

Quox Quietly Quits

WHEN the chief nomes assembled before their new King they joyfully saluted him and promised to obey his commands. But, when Kaliko questioned them, none knew the way to the Metal Forest, although all had assisted in its making. So the King instructed them to search carefully for one of the passages and to bring him the news as soon as they had found it.

Meantime Quox had managed to back out of the rocky corridor and so regain the open air and his old station on the mountain-side, and there he lay upon the rocks, sound asleep, until the next day. The others of the party were all given as good rooms as the caverns of the nomes afforded, for King

213

Kaliko felt that he was indebted to them for his promotion and was anxious to be as hospitable as he could.

Much wonderment had been caused by the absolute disappearance of the sixteen officers of Oogaboo and their Queen. Not a nome had seen them, nor were they discovered during the search for the passages leading to the Metal Forest. Perhaps no one was unhappy over their loss, but all were curious to know what had become of them.

On the next day, when our friends went to visit the dragon, Quox said to them: "I must now bid you good-bye, for my mission here is finished and I must depart for the other side of the world, where I belong."

"Will you go through the Tube again?" asked Betsy.

"To be sure. But it will be a lonely trip this time, with no one to talk to, and I cannot invite any of you to go with me. Therefore, as soon as I slide into the hole I shall go to sleep, and when I pop out at the other end I will wake up at home."

They thanked the dragon for befriending them and wished him a pleasant journey. Also they sent their thanks to the great Jinjin, whose just condemnation of Ruggedo had served their interests so well. Then Quox yawned and stretched himself and ambled over to the Tube, into which he slid headforemost and disappeared.

They really felt as if they had lost a friend, for the dragon had been both kind and sociable during their brief acquaintance with him; but they knew it was his duty to return to his own country. So they went back to the caverns to renew the search for the hidden passages that led to the forest, but for three days all efforts to find them proved in vain.

It was Polychrome's custom to go every day to the mountain and watch for her father, the Rainbow, for she was growing tired with wandering upon the earth and longed to rejoin her sisters in their sky palaces. And on the third day, while she sat motionless upon a point of rock, whom should she see slyly creeping up the mountain but Ruggedo!

The former King looked very forlorn. His clothes were soiled and torn and he had no sandals upon his feet or hat upon his head. Having left his crown and sceptre behind when he fled, the old nome no longer seemed kingly, but more like a beggarman.

Several times had Ruggedo crept up to the mouth of the caverns, only to find the six eggs still on guard. He knew quite well that he must accept his fate and become a homeless wanderer, but his chief regret now was that he had neglected to fill his pockets with gold and jewels. He was aware that a wanderer with wealth at his command would fare much better than one who was a pauper, so he still loitered around the caverns wherein he knew so much treasure was stored, hoping for a chance to fill his pockets.

That was how he came to recollect the Metal Forest.

"Aha!" said he to himself, "I alone know the way to that Forest, and once there I can fill my pockets with the finest jewels in all the world."

He glanced at his pockets and was grieved to find them so small. Perhaps they might be enlarged, so that they would hold more. He knew of a poor woman who lived in a cottage at the foot of the mountain, so he went to her and begged her to sew pockets all over his robe, paying her with the gift of a diamond ring which he had worn upon his finger. The woman was delighted to possess so valuable a ring and she sewed as many pockets on Ruggedo's robe as she possibly could.

Then he returned up the mountain and, after gazing cautiously around to make sure he was not observed, he touched a spring in a rock and it swung slowly backward, disclosing a broad passageway. This he entered, swinging the rock in place behind him.

However, Ruggedo had failed to look as carefully as he might have done, for Polychrome was seated only a little distance off and her clear eyes marked exactly the manner in which Ruggedo had released the hidden spring. So she rose and hurried into the cavern, where she told Kaliko and her friends of her discovery.

"I've no doubt that that is a way to the Metal Forest,"

exclaimed Shaggy. "Come, let us follow Ruggedo at once and rescue my poor brother!"

They agreed to this and King Kaliko called together a band of nomes to assist them by carrying torches to light their way.

"The Metal Forest has a brilliant light of its own," said he, "but the passage across the valley is likely to be dark."

Polychrome easily found the rock and touched the spring, so in less than an hour after Ruggedo had entered they were all in the passage and following swiftly after the former King.

"He means to rob the Forest, I'm sure," said Kaliko; "but he will find he is no longer of any account in this Kingdom and I will have my nomes throw him out."

"Then please throw him as hard as you can," said Betsy, "for he deserves it. I don't mind an honest, out-an'-out enemy, who fights square; but changing girls into fiddles and ordering 'em put into Slimy Caves is mean and tricky, and Ruggedo doesn't deserve any sympathy. But you'll have to let him take as much treasure as he can get in his pockets, Kaliko."

"Yes, the Jinjin said so; but we won't miss it much. There is more treasure in the Metal Forest than a million nomes could carry in their pockets."

It was not difficult to walk through this passage, especially when the torches lighted the way, so they made good progress. But it proved to be a long distance and Betsy had tired herself with walking and was seated upon the back of the mule when the passage made a sharp turn and a wonderful and glorious light burst upon them. The next moment they were all standing upon the edge of the marvelous Metal Forest.

It lay under another mountain and occupied a great domed cavern, the roof of which was higher than a church steeple. In this space the industrious nomes had built, during many years of labor, the most beautiful forest in the world. The trees—trunks, branches and leaves—were all of solid gold, while the bushes and underbrush were formed of filigree silver, virgin pure. The trees towered as high as natural live oaks do and were of exquisite workmanship.

On the ground were thickly strewn precious gems of every hue and size, while here and there among the trees were paths pebbled with cut diamonds of the clearest water. Taken all together, more treasure was gathered in this Metal Forest than is contained in all the rest of the world—if we except the land of Oz, where perhaps its value is equalled in the famous Emerald City.

Our friends were so amazed at the sight that for a while they stood gazing in silent wonder. Then Shaggy exclaimed:

"My brother! My dear lost brother! Is he indeed a prisoner in this place?"

"Yes," replied Kaliko. "The Ugly One has been here for two or three years, to my positive knowledge."

"But what could he find to eat?" inquired Betsy. "It's an awfully swell place to live in, but one can't breakfast on rubies and di'monds, or even gold."

"One doesn't need to, my dear," Kaliko assured her. "The Metal Forest does not fill all of this great cavern, by any means. Beyond these gold and silver trees are other trees of the real sort, which bear foods very nice to eat. Let us walk in that direction, for I am quite sure we will find Shaggy's brother in that part of the cavern, rather than in this."

So they began to tramp over the diamond-pebbled paths, and at every step they were more and more bewildered by the wondrous beauty of the golden trees with their glittering foliage.

Suddenly they heard a scream. Jewels scattered in every direction as some one hidden among the bushes scampered away before them. Then a loud voice cried: "Halt!" and there was the sound of a struggle.

CHAPTER 21

A Bashful Brother

WITH fast beating hearts they all rushed forward and, beyond a group of stately metal trees, came full upon a most astonishing scene.

There was Ruggedo in the hands of the officers of Ooga-boo, a dozen of whom were clinging to the old nome and holding him fast in spite of his efforts to escape. There also was Queen Ann, looking grimly upon the scene of strife; but when she observed her former companions approaching she turned away in a shamefaced manner.

For Ann and her officers were indeed a sight to behold. Her Majesty's clothing, once so rich and gorgeous, was now worn and torn into shreds by her long crawl through the tunnel, which, by the way, had led her directly into the Metal Forest. It was, indeed, one of the three secret passages, and by far the most difficult of the three. Ann had not only torn her pretty skirt and jacket, but her crown had become bent and battered and even her shoes were so cut and slashed that they were ready to fall from her feet.

The officers had fared somewhat worse than their leader, for holes were worn in the knees of their trousers, while sharp points of rock in the roof and sides of the tunnel had made rags of every inch of their once brilliant uniforms. A more tattered and woeful army never came out of a battle, than these harmless victims of the rocky passage. But it had seemed their only means of escape from the cruel Nome King; so they had crawled on, regardless of their sufferings.

When they reached the Metal Forest their eyes beheld more plunder than they had ever dreamed of; yet they were prisoners in this huge dome and could not escape with the riches heaped about them. Perhaps a more unhappy and homesick lot of "conquerors" never existed than this band from Oogaboo.

After several days of wandering in their marvelous prison they were frightened by the discovery that Ruggedo had come among them. Rendered desperate by their sad condition, the officers exhibited courage for the first time since they left home and, ignorant of the fact that Ruggedo was no longer King of the nomes, they threw themselves upon him and had just succeeded in capturing him when their fellow adventurers reached the spot.

"Goodness gracious!" cried Betsy. "What has happened to you all?"

Ann came forward to greet them, sorrowful and indignant.

"We were obliged to escape from the pit through a small tunnel, which was lined with sharp and jagged rocks," said she, "and not only was our clothing torn to rags but our flesh is so bruised and sore that we are stiff and lame in every joint. To add to our troubles we find we are still prisoners; but now that we have succeeded in capturing the wicked Metal Monarch we shall force him to grant us our liberty."

"Ruggedo is no longer Metal Monarch, or King of the nomes," Files informed her. "He has been deposed and cast out of his kingdom by Quox; but here is the new King, whose name is Kaliko, and I am pleased to assure Your Majesty that he is our friend."

"Glad to meet Your Majesty, I'm sure," said Kaliko, bowing as courteously as if the Queen still wore splendid raiment.

The officers, having heard this explanation, now set Ruggedo free; but, as he had no place to go, he stood by and faced his former servant, who was now King in his place, in a humble and pleading manner.

"What are you doing here?" asked Kaliko sternly.

"Why, I was promised as much treasure as I could carry in my pockets," replied Ruggedo; "so I came here to get it, not wishing to disturb Your Majesty."

"You were commanded to leave the country of the nomes forever!" declared Kaliko.

"I know; and I'll go as soon as I have filled my pockets," said Ruggedo, meekly.

"Then fill them, and be gone," returned the new King.

Ruggedo obeyed. Stooping down, he began gathering up jewels by the handful and stuffing them into his many pockets. They were heavy things, these diamonds and rubies and emeralds and amethysts and the like, so before long Ruggedo was staggering with the weight he bore, while the pockets were not yet filled. When he could no longer stoop over without falling, Betsy and Polychrome and the Rose Princess came to his assistance, picking up the finest gems and tucking them into his pockets.

At last these were all filled and Ruggedo presented a comical sight, for surely no man ever before had so many pockets, or any at all filled with such a choice collection of precious stones. He neglected to thank the young ladies for their kindness, but gave them a surly nod of farewell and staggered down the path by the way he had come. They let him depart in silence, for with all he had taken, the masses of jewels upon the ground seemed scarcely to have

been disturbed, so numerous were they. Also they hoped they had seen the last of the degraded King.

"I'm awful glad he's gone," said Betsy, sighing deeply. "If he doesn't get reckless and spend his wealth foolishly, he's got enough to start a bank when he gets to Oklahoma."

"But my brother—my dear brother! Where is he?" inquired Shaggy anxiously. "Have you seen him, Queen Ann?"

"What does your brother look like?" asked the Queen.

Shaggy hesitated to reply, but Betsy said: "He's called the Ugly One. Perhaps you'll know him by that."

"The only person we have seen in this cavern," said Ann, "has run away from us whenever we approached him. He hides over yonder, among the trees that are not gold, and we have never been able to catch sight of his face. So I cannot tell whether he is ugly or not."

"That must be my dear brother!" exclaimed Shaggy.

"Yes, it must be," assented Kaliko. "No one else inhabits this splendid dome, so there can be no mistake."

"But why does he hide among those green trees, instead of enjoying all these glittery golden ones?" asked Betsy.

"Because he finds food among the natural trees," replied Kaliko, "and I remember that he has built a little house there, to sleep in. As for these glittery golden trees, I will admit they are very pretty at first sight. One cannot fail to admire them, as well as the rich jewels scattered beneath them; but if one has to look at them always, they become pretty tame."

"I believe that is true," declared Shaggy. "My dear brother is very wise to prefer real trees to the imitation ones. But come; let us go there and find him."

Shaggy started for the green grove at once, and the others followed him, being curious to witness the final rescue of his long-sought, long-lost brother.

Not far from the edge of the grove they came upon a small hut, cleverly made of twigs and golden branches woven together. As they approached the place they caught a glimpse of a form that darted into the hut and slammed the door tight shut after him.

Shaggy Man ran to the door and cried aloud:

"Brother! Brother!"

"Who calls," demanded a sad, hollow voice from within.

"It is Shaggy—your own loving brother—who has been searching for you a long time and has now come to rescue you."

"Too late!" replied the gloomy voice. "No one can rescue me now."

"Oh, but you are mistaken about that," said Shaggy. "There is a new King of the nomes, named Kaliko, in Ruggedo's place, and he has promised you shall go free."

227

"Free! I dare not go free!" said the Ugly One, in a voice of despair.

"Why not, Brother?" asked Shaggy, anxiously.

"Do you know what they have done to me?" came the answer through the closed door.

"No. Tell me, Brother, what have they done?"

"When Ruggedo first captured me I was very handsome. Don't you remember, Shaggy?"

"Not very well, Brother; you were so young when I left home. But I remember that mother thought you were beautiful."

"She was right! I am sure she was right," wailed the prisoner. "But Ruggedo wanted to injure me—to make me ugly in the eyes of all the world—so he performed a wicked enchantment. I went to bed beautiful—or you might say handsome—to be very modest I will merely claim that I was good-looking—and I wakened the next morning the homeliest man in all the world! I am so repulsive that when I look in a mirror I frighten myself."

"Poor Brother!" said Shaggy softly, and all the others were silent from sympathy.

"I was so ashamed of my looks," continued the voice of Shaggy's brother, "that I tried to hide; but the cruel King Ruggedo forced me to appear before all the legion of nomes, to whom he said: 'Behold the Ugly One!' But when the nomes saw my face they all fell to laughing and jeering, which prevented them from working at their tasks. Seeing this, Ruggedo became angry and pushed me into a tunnel, closing the rock entrance so that I could not get out. I followed the length of the tunnel until I reached this huge dome, where the marvelous Metal Forest stands, and here I have remained ever since."

"Poor Brother!" repeated Shaggy. "But I beg you now to come forth and face us, who are your friends. None here will laugh or jeer, however unhandsome you may be."

"No, indeed," they all added pleadingly.

But the Ugly One refused the invitation.

"I cannot," said he; "indeed, I cannot face strangers, ugly as I am."

Shaggy Man turned to the group surrounding him.

"What shall I do?" he asked in sorrowful tones. "I cannot leave my dear brother here, and he refuses to come out of that house and face us."

"I'll tell you," replied Betsy. "Let him put on a mask."

"The very idea I was seeking!" exclaimed Shaggy joyfully; and then he called out: "Brother, put a mask over your face, and then none of us can see what your features are like."

"I have no mask," answered the Ugly One.

"Look here," said Betsy; "he can use my handkerchief."

Shaggy looked at the little square of cloth and shook his head.

"It isn't big enough," he objected; "I'm sure it isn't big enough to hide a man's face. But he can use mine."

Saying this he took from his pocket his own handkerchief and went to the door of the hut.

"Here, my Brother," he called, "take this handkerchief and make a mask of it. I will also pass you my knife, so that you may cut holes for the eyes, and then you must tie it over your face."

The door slowly opened, just far enough for the Ugly One to thrust out his hand and take the handkerchief and the knife. Then it closed again.

"Don't forget a hole for your nose," cried Betsy. "You must breathe, you know."

For a time there was silence. Queen Ann and her army sat down upon the ground to rest. Betsy sat on Hank's back. Polychrome danced lightly up and down the jeweled paths while Files and the Princess wandered through the groves arm in arm. Tik-Tok, who never tired, stood motionless.

By and by a noise sounded from within the hut.

"Are you ready?" asked Shaggy.

"Yes, Brother," came the reply, and the door was thrown open to allow the Ugly One to step forth.

Betsy might have laughed aloud had she not remembered

230

how sensitive to ridicule Shaggy's brother was, for the handkerchief with which he had masked his features was a red one covered with big white polka dots. In this two holes had been cut—in front of the eyes—while two smaller ones before the nostrils allowed the man to breathe freely. The cloth was then tightly drawn over the Ugly One's face and knotted at the back of his neck.

He was dressed in clothes that had once been good, but now were sadly worn and frayed. His silk stockings had holes in them, and his shoes were stub-toed and needed blackening. "But what can you expect," whispered Betsy, "when the poor man has been a prisoner for so many years?"

Shaggy had darted forward, and embraced his newly found brother with both his arms. The brother also embraced Shaggy, who then led him forward and introduced him to all the assembled company.

"This is the new Nome King," he said when he came to Kaliko. "He is our friend, and has granted you your freedom."

"That is a kindly deed," replied Ugly in a sad voice, "but I dread to go back to the world in this direful condition. Unless I remain forever masked, my dreadful face would curdle all the milk and stop all the clocks."

"Can't the enchantment be broken in some way?" inquired Betsy.

Shaggy looked anxiously at Kaliko, who shook his head.

"I am sure *I* can't break the enchantment," he said. "Ruggedo was fond of magic, and learned a good many enchantments that we nomes know nothing of."

"Perhaps Ruggedo himself might break his own enchantment," suggested Ann; "but unfortunately we have allowed the old King to escape."

"Never mind, my dear Brother," said Shaggy consolingly; "I am very happy to have found you again, although I may never see your face. So let us make the most of this joyful reunion."

The Ugly One was affected to tears by this tender speech, and the tears began to wet the red handkerchief; so Shaggy gently wiped them away with his coat sleeve.

CHAPTER 22

Kindly Kisses

"WON'T you be dreadful sorry to leave this lovely place?" Betsy asked the Ugly One.

"No, indeed," said he. "Jewels and gold are cold and heartless things, and I am sure I would presently have died of loneliness had I not found this natural forest at the edge of the artificial one. Anyhow, without these real trees I should soon have starved to death."

Betsy looked around at the quaint trees.

"I don't just understand that," she admitted. "What could you find to eat here,"

"The best food in the world," Ugly answered. "Do you see that grove at your left?" he added, pointing it out; "well, such trees as those do not grow in your country, or in any other place but this cavern. I have named them 'Hotel Trees,' because they bear a certain kind of table d'hote fruit called 'Three-Course Nuts.' "

"That's funny!" said Betsy. "What are the 'Three-Course Nuts' like?"

"Something like cocoanuts, to look at," explained the Ugly One. "All you have to do is to pick one of them and then sit down and eat your dinner. You first unscrew the top part and find a cupfull of good soup. After you've eaten that, you unscrew the middle part and find a hollow filled with meat and potatoes, vegetables and a fine salad. Eat that, and unscrew the next section, and you come to the dessert in the bottom of the nut. That is pie and cake, cheese and crackers, and nuts and raisins. The Three-Course Nuts are not all exactly alike in flavor or in contents, but they are all good and in each one may be found a complete three-course dinner."

"But how about breakfasts?" inquired Betsy.

"Why, there are Breakfast Trees for that, which grow over there at the right. They bear nuts, like the others, only the nuts contain coffee or chocolate, instead of soup; oatmeal instead of meat-and-potatoes, and fruits instead of dessert. Sad as has been my life in this wonderful prison, I must admit that no one could live more luxuriously in the best hotel in the world than I have lived here; but I will be glad to get into the open air again and see the good old sun and the silvery moon and the soft green grass and the flowers that are kissed by the morning dew. Ah, how much more lovely are those blessed things than the glitter of gems or the cold gleam of gold!"

"Of course," said Betsy. "I once knew a little boy who wanted to catch the measles, because all the little boys in his neighborhood but him had had 'em, and he was really unhappy 'cause he couldn't catch 'em, try as he would. So I'm pretty certain that the things we want, and can't have, are not good for us. Isn't that true, Shaggy?"

"Not always, my dear," he gravely replied. "If we didn't want anything, we would never get anything, good or bad. I think our longings are natural, and if we act as nature prompts us we can't go far wrong."

"For my part," said Queen Ann, "I think the world would be a dreary place without the gold and jewels."

"All things are good in their way," said Shaggy; "but we may have too much of any good thing. And I have noticed that the value of anything depends upon how scarce it is, and how difficult it is to obtain."

"Pardon me for interrupting you," said King Kaliko, coming to their side, "but now that we have rescued Shaggy's brother I would like to return to my royal cavern. Being the

King of the Nomes, it is my duty to look after my restless subjects and see that they behave themselves."

So they all turned and began walking through the Metal Forest to the other side of the great domed cave, where they had first entered it. Shaggy and his brother walked side by side and both seemed rejoiced that they were together after their long separation. Betsy didn't dare look at the polka-dot handkerchief, for fear she would laugh aloud; so she walked behind the two brothers and led Hank by holding fast to his left ear.

When at last they reached the place where the passage led to the outer world, Queen Ann said, in a hesitating way that was unusual with her:

"I have not conquered this Nome Country, nor do I expect to do so; but I would like to gather a few of these pretty jewels before I leave this place."

"Help yourself, ma'am," said King Kaliko, and at once the officers of the Army took advantage of his royal permission and began filling their pockets, while Ann tied a lot of diamonds in a big handkerchief.

This accomplished, they all entered the passage, the nomes going first to light the way with their torches. They had not proceeded far when Betsy exclaimed:

"Why, there are jewels here, too!"

All eyes were turned upon the ground and they found a

regular trail of jewels strewn along the rock floor.

"This is queer!" said Kaliko, much surprised. "I must send some of my nomes to gather up these gems and replace them in the Metal Forest, where they belong. I wonder how they came to be here?"

All the way along the passage they found this trail of jewels, but when they neared the end the mystery was explained. For there, squatted upon the floor with his back to the rock wall, sat old Ruggedo, puffing and blowing as if he was all tired out. Then they realized it was he who had scattered the jewels, from his many pockets, which one by one had burst with the weight of their contents as he had stumbled along the passage.

"But I don't mind," said Ruggedo, with a deep sigh. "I now realize that I could not have carried such a weighty load very far, even had I managed to escape from this passage with it. The woman who sewed the pockets on my robe used poor thread, for which I shall thank her."

"Have you any jewels left?" inquired Betsy.

He glanced into some of the remaining pockets.

"A few," said he, "but they will be sufficient to supply my wants, and I no longer have any desire to be rich. If some of you will kindly help me to rise, I'll get out of here and leave you, for I know you all despise me and prefer my room to my company."

Shaggy and Kaliko raised the old King to his feet, when he was confronted by Shaggy's brother, whom he now noticed for the first time. The queer and unexpected appearance of the Ugly One so startled Ruggedo that he gave a wild cry and began to tremble, as if he had seen a ghost.

"Wh—wh—who is this?" he faltered.

"I am that helpless prisoner whom your cruel magic transformed from a handsome man into an ugly one!" answered Shaggy's brother, in a voice of stern reproach.

"Really, Ruggedo," said Betsy, "you ought to be ashamed of that mean trick."

"I am, my dear," admitted Ruggedo, who was now as meek and humble as formerly he had been cruel and vindictive.

"Then," returned the girl, "you'd better do some more magic and give the poor man his own face again."

"I wish I could," answered the old King; "but you must remember that Tititi-Hoochoo has deprived me of all my magic powers. However, I never took the trouble to learn just how to break the charm I cast over Shaggy's brother, for I intended he should always remain ugly."

"Every charm," remarked pretty Polychrome, "has its antidote; and, if you knew this charm of ugliness, Ruggedo, you must have known how to dispel it."

He shook his head.

"If I did, I—I've forgotten," he stammered regretfully.

"Try to think!" pleaded Shaggy, anxiously. "*Please* try to think!"

Ruggedo ruffled his hair with both hands, sighed, slapped his chest, rubbed his ear, and stared stupidly around the group.

"I've a faint recollection that there *was* one thing that would break the charm," said he; "but misfortune has so addled my brain that I can't remember what it was."

"See here, Ruggedo," said Betsy, sharply, "we've treated you pretty well, so far, but we won't stand for any nonsense, and if you know what's good for yourself you'll think of that charm!"

"Why?" he demanded, turning to look wonderingly at the little girl.

"Because it means so much to Shaggy's brother. He's dreadfully ashamed of himself, the way he is now, and you're to blame for it. Fact is, Ruggedo, you've done so much wickedness in your life that it won't hurt you to do a kind act now."

Ruggedo blinked at her, and sighed again, and then tried very hard to think.

"I seem to remember, dimly," said he, "that a certain kind of a kiss will break the charm of ugliness."

"What kind of a kiss?"

Chapter Twenty-Two

"What kind? Why, it was— it was— it was either the kiss of a Mortal Maid; or— or— the kiss of a Mortal Maid who had once been a Fairy; or— or the kiss of one who is still a Fairy. I can't remember which. But of course no maid, mortal or fairy, would ever consent to kiss a person so ugly —so dreadfully, fearfully, terribly ugly—as Shaggy's brother."

"I'm not so sure of that," said Betsy, with admirable courage; "I'm a Mortal Maid, and if it is *my* kiss that will break this awful charm, I—I'll do it!"

"Oh, you really couldn't," protested Ugly. "I would be obliged to remove my mask, and when you saw my face, nothing could induce you to kiss me, generous as you are."

"Well, as for that," said the little girl, "I needn't see your face at all. Here's my plan: You stay in this dark passage, and we'll send away the nomes with their torches. Then you'll take off the handkerchief, and I—I'll kiss you."

"This is awfully kind of you, Betsy!" said Shaggy, gratefully.

"Well, it surely won't kill me," she replied; "and, if it makes you and your brother happy, I'm willing to take some chances."

So Kaliko ordered the torch-bearers to leave the passage, which they did by going through the rock opening. Queen Ann and her army also went out; but the others were so interested in Betsy's experiment that they remained grouped at the mouth of the passageway. When the big rock swung into place, closing tight the opening, they were left in total darkness.

"Now, then," called Betsy in a cheerful voice, "have you got that handkerchief off your face, Ugly?"

"Yes," he replied..

"Well, where are you, then?" she asked, reaching out her arms.

"Here," said he.

"You'll have to stoop down, you know."

He found her hands and clasping them in his own stooped until his face was near to that of the little girl. The others heard a clear, smacking kiss, and then Betsy exclaimed:

"There! I've done it, and it didn't hurt a bit!"

"Tell me, dear brother; is the charm broken?" asked Shaggy.

"I do not know," was the reply. "It may be, or it may not be. I cannot tell."

"Has anyone a match?" inquired Betsy.

"I have several," said Shaggy.

"Then let Ruggedo strike one of them and look at your brother's face, while we all turn our backs. Ruggedo made your brother ugly, so I guess he can stand the horror of looking at him, if the charm isn't broken."

Chapter Twenty-Two

Agreeing to this, Ruggedo took the match and lighted it. He gave one look and then blew out the match.

"Ugly as ever!" he said with a shudder. "So it wasn't the kiss of a Mortal Maid, after all."

"Let me try," proposed the Rose Princess, in her sweet voice. "I am a Mortal Maid who was once a Fairy. Perhaps my kiss will break the charm."

Files did not wholly approve of this, but he was too generous to interfere. So the Rose Princess felt her way through the darkness to Shaggy's brother and kissed him.

Ruggedo struck another match, while they all turned away.

"No," announced the former King; "that didn't break the charm, either. It must be the kiss of a Fairy that is required —or else my memory has failed me altogether."

"Polly," said Betsy, pleadingly, "won't *you* try?"

"Of course I will!" answered Polychrome, with a merry laugh. "I've never kissed a mortal man in all the thousands of years I have existed, but I'll do it to please our faithful Shaggy Man, whose unselfish affection for his ugly brother deserves to be rewarded."

Even as Polychrome was speaking she tripped lightly to the side of the Ugly One and quickly touched his cheek with her lips.

"Oh, thank you—thank you!" he fervently cried. "I've

changed, this time, I know. I can feel it! I'm different. Shaggy—dear Shaggy—I am myself again!"

Files, who was near the opening, touched the spring that released the big rock and it suddenly swung backward and let in a flood of daylight.

Everyone stood motionless, staring hard at Shaggy's brother, who, no longer masked by the polka-dot handkerchief, met their gaze with a glad smile.

"Well," said Shaggy Man, breaking the silence at last and drawing a long, deep breath of satisfaction, "you are no longer the Ugly One, my dear brother; but, to be entirely frank with you, the face that belongs to you is no more handsome than it ought to be."

"I think he's rather good looking," remarked Betsy, gazing at the man critically.

"In comparison with what he was," said King Kaliko, "he is really beautiful. You, who never beheld his ugliness, may not understand that; but it was my misfortune to look at the Ugly One many times, and I say again that, in comparison with what he was, the man is now beautiful."

"All right," returned Betsy, briskly, "we'll take your word for it, Kaliko. And now let us get out of this tunnel and into the world again."

CHAPTER 23

Ruggedo Reforms

IT DID not take them long to regain the royal cavern of the Nome King, where Kaliko ordered served to them the nicest refreshments the place afforded.

Ruggedo had come trailing along after the rest of the party and while no one paid any attention to the old King they did not offer any objection to his presence or command him to leave them. He looked fearfully to see if the eggs were still guarding the entrance, but they had now disappeared; so he crept into the cavern after the others and humbly squatted down in a corner of the room.

There Betsy discovered him. All of the little girl's companions were now so happy at the success of Shaggy's quest

245

for his brother, and the laughter and merriment seemed so general, that Betsy's heart softened toward the friendless old man who had once been their bitter enemy, and she carried to him some of the food and drink.

Ruggedo's eyes filled with tears at this unexpected kindness. He took the child's hand in his own and pressed it gratefully.

"Look here, Kaliko," said Betsy, addressing the new King, "what's the use of being hard on Ruggedo? All his magic power is gone, so he can't do any more harm, and I'm sure he's sorry he acted so badly to everybody."

"Are you?" asked Kaliko, looking down at his former master.

"I am," said Ruggedo. "The girl speaks truly. I'm sorry and I'm harmless. I don't want to wander through the wide world, on top of the ground, for I'm a nome. No nome can ever be happy any place but underground."

"That being the case," said Kaliko, "I will let you stay here as long as you behave yourself; but, if you try to act badly again, I shall drive you out, as Tititi-Hoochoo has commanded, and you'll have to wander."

"Never fear. I'll behave," promised Ruggedo. "It is hard work being a King, and harder still to be a good King. But now that I am a common nome I am sure I can lead a blameless life."

Chapter Twenty-Three

They were all pleased to hear this and to know that Ruggedo had really reformed.

"I hope he'll keep his word," whispered Betsy to Shaggy; "but if he gets bad again we will be far away from the Nome Kingdom and Kaliko will have to 'tend to the old nome himself."

Polychrome had been a little restless during the last hour or two. The lovely Daughter of the Rainbow knew that she had now done all in her power to assist her earth friends, and so she began to long for her sky home.

"I think," she said, after listening intently, "that it is beginning to rain. The Rain King is my uncle, you know, and perhaps he has read my thoughts and is going to help me. Anyway, I must take a look at the sky and make sure."

So she jumped up and ran through the passage to the outer entrance, and they all followed after her and grouped themselves on a ledge of the mountain-side. Sure enough, dark clouds had filled the sky and a slow, drizzling rain had set in.

"It can't last for long," said Shaggy, looking upward, "and when it stops we shall lose the sweet little fairy we have learned to love. Alas," he continued, after a moment, "the clouds are already breaking in the west, and—see!—isn't that the Rainbow coming?"

Betsy didn't look at the sky; she looked at Polychrome,

247

whose happy, smiling face surely foretold the coming of her father to take her to the Cloud Palaces. A moment later a gleam of sunshine flooded the mountain and a gorgeous Rainbow appeared.

With a cry of gladness Polychrome sprang upon a point of rock and held out her arms. Straightway the Rainbow descended until its end was at her very feet, when with a graceful leap she sprang upon it and was at once clasped in the arms of her radiant sisters, the Daughters of the Rainbow. But Polychrome released herself to lean over the edge of the glowing arch and nod, and smile and throw a dozen kisses to her late comrades.

"Good-bye!" she called, and they all shouted "Good-bye!" in return and waved their hands to their pretty friend.

Slowly the magnificent bow lifted and melted into the sky, until the eyes of the earnest watchers saw only fleecy clouds flitting across the blue.

"I'm dreadful sorry to see Polychrome go," said Betsy, who felt like crying; "but I s'pose she'll be a good deal happier with her sisters in the sky palaces."

"To be sure," returned Shaggy, nodding gravely. "It's her home, you know, and those poor wanderers who, like ourselves, have no home, can realize what that means to her."

"Once," said Betsy, "I, too, had a home. Now, I've only —only—dear old Hank!"

She twined her arms around her shaggy friend who was not human, and he said: "Hee-haw!" in a tone that showed he understood her mood. And the shaggy friend who was human stroked the child's head tenderly and said: "You're wrong about that, Betsy dear. I will never desert you."

"Nor I!" exclaimed Shaggy's brother, in earnest tones.

The little girl looked up at them gratefully, and her eyes smiled through their tears.

"All right," she said. "It's raining again, so let's go back into the cavern."

Rather soberly, for all loved Polychrome and would miss her, they reëntered the dominions of the Nome King.

CHAPTER 24

Dorothy is Delighted

"WELL," said Queen Ann, when all were again seated in Kaliko's royal cavern, "I wonder what we shall do next. If I could find my way back to Oogaboo I'd take my army home at once, for I'm sick and tired of these dreadful hardships."

"Don't you want to conquer the world?" asked Betsy.

"No; I've changed my mind about that," admitted the Queen. "The world is too big for one person to conquer and I was happier with my own people in Oogaboo. I wish— Oh, how earnestly I wish—that I was back there this minute!"

"So do I!" yelled every officer in a fervent tone.

Now, it is time for the reader to know that in the far-away Land of Oz the lovely Ruler, Ozma, had been following the adventures of her Shaggy Man, and Tik-Tok, and all the others they had met. Day by day Ozma, with the wonderful Wizard of Oz seated beside her, had gazed upon a Magic Picture in a radium frame, which occupied one side of the Ruler's cosy boudoir in the palace of the Emerald City. The singular thing about this Magic Picture was that it showed whatever scene Ozma wished to see, with the figures all in motion, just as it was taking place. So Ozma and the Wizard had watched every action of the adventurers from the time Shaggy had met shipwrecked Betsy and Hank in the Rose Kingdom, at which time the Rose Princess, a distant cousin of Ozma, had been exiled by her heartless subjects.

When Ann and her people so earnestly wished to return to Oogaboo, Ozma was sorry for them and remembered that Oogaboo was a corner of the Land of Oz. She turned to her attendant and asked:

"Can not your magic take these unhappy people to their old home, Wizard?"

"It can, Your Highness," replied the little Wizard.

"I think the poor Queen has suffered enough in her misguided effort to conquer the world," said Ozma, smiling at the absurdity of the undertaking, "so no doubt she will hereafter be contented in her own little Kingdom. Please send her there, Wizard, and with her the officers and Files."

"How about the Rose Princess?" asked the Wizard.

Chapter Twenty-Four

"Send her to Oogaboo with Files," answered Ozma. "They have become such good friends that I am sure it would make them unhappy to separate them."

"Very well," said the Wizard, and without any fuss or mystery whatever he performed a magical rite that was simple and effective. Therefore those seated in the Nome King's cavern were both startled and amazed when all the people of Oogaboo suddenly disappeared from the room, and with them the Rose Princess. At first they could not understand it at all; but presently Shaggy suspected the truth, and believing that Ozma was now taking an interest in the party he drew from his pocket a tiny instrument which he placed against his ear.

Ozma, observing this action in her Magic Picture, at once caught up a similar instrument from a table beside her and held it to her own ear. The two instruments recorded the same delicate vibrations of sound and formed a wireless telephone, an invention of the Wizard. Those separated by any distance were thus enabled to converse together with perfect ease and without any wire connection.

"Do you hear me, Shaggy Man?" asked Ozma.

"Yes, Your Highness," he replied.

"I have sent the people of Oogaboo back to their own little valley," announced the Ruler of Oz; "so do not worry over their disappearance."

"That was very kind of you," said Shaggy. "But Your Highness must permit me to report that my own mission here is now ended. I have found my lost brother, and he is now beside me, freed from the enchantment of ugliness which Ruggedo cast upon him. Tik-Tok has served me and my comrades faithfully, as you requested him to do, and I hope you will now transport the Clockwork Man back to your fairyland of Oz."

"I will do that," replied Ozma. "But how about yourself, Shaggy?"

"I have been very happy in Oz," he said, "but my duty to others forces me to exile myself from that delightful land. I must take care of my new-found brother, for one thing, and I have a new comrade in a dear little girl named Betsy Bobbin, who has no home to go to, and no other friends but me and a small donkey named Hank. I have promised Betsy never to desert her as long as she needs a friend, and so I must give up the delights of the Land of Oz forever."

He said this with a sigh of regret, and Ozma made no reply but laid the tiny instrument on her table, thus cutting off all further communication with the Shaggy Man. But the lovely Ruler of Oz still watched her magic picture, with a thoughtful expression upon her face, and the little Wizard of Oz watched Ozma and smiled softly to himself.

In the cavern of the Nome King Shaggy replaced the

wireless telephone in his pocket and turning to Betsy said in as cheerful a voice as he could muster:

"Well, little comrade, what shall we do next?"

"I don't know, I'm sure," she answered with a puzzled face. "I'm kind of sorry our adventures are over, for I enjoyed them, and now that Queen Ann and her people are gone, and Polychrome is gone, and—dear me!—where's Tik-Tok, Shaggy?"

"He also has disappeared," said Shaggy, looking around the cavern and nodding wisely. "By this time he is in Ozma's palace in the Land of Oz, which is his home."

"Isn't it your home, too?" asked Betsy.

"It used to be, my dear; but now my home is wherever you and my brother are. We are wanderers, you know, but if we stick together I am sure we shall have a good time."

"Then," said the girl, "let us get out of this stuffy, underground cavern and go in search of new adventures. I'm sure it has stopped raining."

"I'm ready," said Shaggy, and then they bade good-bye to King Kaliko, and thanked him for his assistance, and went out to the mouth of the passage.

The sky was now clear and a brilliant blue in color; the sun shone brightly and even this rugged, rocky country seemed delightful after their confinement underground. There were but four of them now—Betsy and Hank, and

Tik-Tok of Oz

Shaggy and his brother—and the little party made their way down the mountain and followed a faint path that led toward the southwest.

During this time Ozma had been holding a conference with the Wizard, and later with Tik-Tok, whom the magic of the Wizard had quickly transported to Ozma's palace. Tik-Tok had only words of praise for Betsy Bobbin, "who," he said, "is al-most as nice as Dor-o-thy her-self."

"Let us send for Dorothy," said Ozma, and summoning her favorite maid, who was named Jellia Jamb, she asked her to request Princess Dorothy to attend her at once. So a few moments later Dorothy entered Ozma's room and greeted her and the Wizard and Tik-Tok with the same gentle smile and simple manner that had won for the little girl the love of everyone she met.

"Did you want to see me, Ozma?" she asked.

"Yes, dear. I am puzzled how to act, and I want your advice."

"I don't b'lieve it's worth much," replied Dorothy, "but I'll do the best I can. What is it all about, Ozma?"

"You all know," said the girl Ruler, addressing her three friends, "what a serious thing it is to admit any mortals into this fairyland of Oz. It is true I have invited several mortals to make their home here, and all of them have proved true and loyal subjects. Indeed, no one of you three was a native of Oz. Dorothy and the Wizard came here from the United States, and Tik-Tok came from the Land of Ev. But of course he is not a mortal. Shaggy is another American, and he is the cause of all my worry, for our dear Shaggy will not return here and desert the new friends he has found in his recent adventures, because he believes they need his services."

"Shaggy Man was always kind-hearted," remarked Dorothy. "But who are these new friends he has found?"

"One is his brother, who for many years has been a prisoner of the Nome King, our old enemy Ruggedo. This brother seems a kindly, honest fellow, but he has done nothing to entitle him to a home in the Land of Oz."

"Who else?" asked Dorothy.

"I have told you about Betsy Bobbin, the little girl who was shipwrecked—in much the same way you once were—and has since been following the Shaggy Man in his search for his lost brother. You remember her, do you not?"

"Oh, yes!" exclaimed Dorothy. "I've often watched her and Hank in the Magic Picture, you know. She's a dear little girl, and old Hank is a darling! Where are they now?"

"Look and see," replied Ozma with a smile at her friend's enthusiasm.

Dorothy turned to the picture, which showed Betsy and Hank, with Shaggy and his brother, trudging along the rocky paths of a barren country.

"Seems to me," she said, musingly, "that they're a good way from any place to sleep, or any nice things to eat."

"You are right," said Tik-Tok. "I have been in that coun-try, and it is a wil-der-ness."

"It is the country of the nomes," explained the Wizard, "who are so mischievous that no one cares to live near them. I'm afraid Shaggy and his friends will endure many hardships before they get out of that rocky place, unless—"

He turned to Ozma and smiled.

"Unless I ask you to transport them all here?" she asked.

"Yes, your Highness."

"Could your magic do that?" inquired Dorothy.

"I think so," said the Wizard.

"Well," said Dorothy, "as far as Betsy and Hank are concerned, I'd like to have them here in Oz. It would be such fun to have a girl playmate of my own age, you see. And Hank is such a dear little mule!"

Ozma laughed at the wistful expression in the girl's eyes, and then she drew Dorothy to her and kissed her.

"Am I not your friend and playmate?" she asked.

Dorothy flushed.

"You know how dearly I love you, Ozma!" she cried. "But you're so busy ruling all this Land of Oz that we can't always be together."

"I know, dear. My first duty is to my subjects, and I

think it would be a delight to us all to have Betsy with us. There's a pretty suite of rooms just opposite your own where she can live, and I'll build a golden stall for Hank in the stable where the Sawhorse lives. Then we'll introduce the mule to the Cowardly Lion and the Hungry Tiger, and I'm sure they will soon become firm friends. But I cannot very well admit Betsy and Hank into Oz unless I also admit Shaggy's brother."

"And, unless you admit Shaggy's brother, you will keep out poor Shaggy, whom we are all very fond of," said the Wizard.

"Well, why not ad-mit him?" demanded Tik-Tok.

"The Land of Oz is not a refuge for all mortals in distress," explained Ozma. "I do not wish to be unkind to Shaggy Man, but his brother has no claim on me."

"The Land of Oz isn't crowded," suggested Dorothy.

"Then you advise me to admit Shaggy's brother?" inquired Ozma.

"Well, we can't afford to lose our Shaggy Man, can we?"

"No, indeed!" returned Ozma. "What do you say, Wizard?"

"I'm getting my magic ready to transport them all."

"And you, Tik-Tok?"

"Shag-gy's broth-er is a good fel-low, and we can't spare Shag-gy."

"So, then, the question is settled," decided Ozma. "Perform your magic, Wizard!"

He did so, placing a silver plate upon a small standard and pouring upon the plate a small quantity of pink powder which was contained in a crystal vial. Then he muttered a rather difficult incantation which the sorceress Glinda the Good had taught him, and it all ended in a puff of perfumed smoke from the silver plate. This smoke was so pungent that it made both Ozma and Dorothy rub their eyes for a moment.

"You must pardon these disagreeable fumes," said the Wizard. "I assure you the smoke is a very necessary part of my wizardry."

"Look!" cried Dorothy, pointing to the Magic Picture; "they're gone! All of them are gone."

Indeed, the picture now showed the same rocky landscape as before, but the three people and the mule had disappeared from it.

"They are gone," said the Wizard, polishing the silver plate and wrapping it in a fine cloth, "because they are here."

At that moment Jellia Jamb entered the room.

"Your Highness," she said to Ozma, "the Shaggy Man and another man are in the waiting room and ask to pay their respects to you. Shaggy is crying like a baby, but he says they are tears of joy."

"Send them here at once, Jellia!" commanded Ozma.

"Also," continued the maid, "a girl and a small-sized mule have mysteriously arrived, but they don't seem to know where they are or how they came here. Shall I send them here, too?"

"Oh, no!" exclaimed Dorothy, eagerly jumping up from her chair; "I'll go to meet Betsy myself, for she'll feel awful strange in this big palace."

And she ran down the stairs two at a time to greet her new friend, Betsy Bobbin.

CHAPTER 25

The Land of Love

"WELL, is 'hee-haw' all you are able to say?" inquired the Sawhorse, as he examined Hank with his knot eyes and slowly wagged the branch that served him for a tail.

They were in a beautiful stable in the rear of Ozma's palace, where the wooden Sawhorse—very much alive—lived in a gold-paneled stall, and where there were rooms for the Cowardly Lion and the Hungry Tiger, which were filled with soft cushions for them to lie upon and golden troughs for them to eat from.

Beside the stall of the Sawhorse had been placed another for Hank, the mule. This was not quite so beautiful as the other, for the Sawhorse was Ozma's favorite steed; but Hank

263

had a supply of cushions for a bed (which the Sawhorse did not need because he never slept) and all this luxury was so strange to the little mule that he could only stand still and regard his surroundings and his queer companions with wonder and amazement.

The Cowardly Lion, looking very dignified, was stretched out upon the marble floor of the stable, eyeing Hank with a calm and critical gaze, while near by crouched the huge Hungry Tiger, who seemed equally interested in the new animal that had just arrived. The Sawhorse, standing stiffly before Hank, repeated his question:

"Is 'hee-haw' all you are able to say?"

Hank moved his ears in an embarrassed manner.

"I have never said anything else, until now," he replied; and then he began to tremble with fright to hear himself talk.

"I can well understand that," remarked the Lion, wagging his great head with a swaying motion. "Strange things happen in this Land of Oz, as they do everywhere else. I believe you came here from the cold, civilized, outside world, did you not?"

"I did," replied Hank. "One minute I was outside of Oz —and the next minute I was inside! That was enough to give me a nervous shock, as you may guess; but to find myself able to talk, as Betsy does, is a marvel that staggers me."

"That is because you are in the Land of Oz," said the

Sawhorse. "All animals talk, in this favored country, and you must admit it is more sociable than to bray your dreadful 'hee-haw,' which nobody can understand."

"Mules understand it very well," declared Hank.

"Oh, indeed! Then there must be other mules in your outside world," said the Tiger, yawning sleepily.

"There are a great many in America," said Hank. "Are you the only Tiger in Oz?"

"No," acknowledged the Tiger, "I have many relatives living in the Jungle Country; but I am the only Tiger living in the Emerald City."

"There are other Lions, too," said the Sawhorse; "but I am the only horse, of any description, in this favored Land."

"That is why this Land is favored," said the Tiger. "You must understand, friend Hank, that the Sawhorse puts on airs because he is shod with plates of gold, and because our beloved Ruler, Ozma of Oz, likes to ride upon his back."

"Betsy rides upon *my* back," declared Hank proudly.

"Who is Betsy?"

"The dearest, sweetest girl in all the world!"

The Sawhorse gave an angry snort and stamped his golden feet. The Tiger crouched and growled. Slowly the great Lion rose to his feet, his mane bristling.

"Friend Hank," said he, "either you are mistaken in judgment or you are willfully trying to deceive us. The dearest, sweetest girl in the world is our Dorothy, and I will fight anyone—animal or human—who dares to deny it!"

"So will I!" snarled the Tiger, showing two rows of enormous white teeth.

"You are all wrong!" asserted the Sawhorse in a voice of scorn. "No girl living can compare with my mistress, Ozma of Oz!"

Hank slowly turned around until his heels were toward the others. Then he said stubbornly:

"I am not mistaken in my statement, nor will I admit there can be a sweeter girl alive than Betsy Bobbin. If you want to fight, come on—I'm ready for you!"

While they hesitated, eyeing Hank's heels doubtfully, a merry peal of laughter startled the animals and turning their heads they beheld three lovely girls standing just within the richly carved entrance to the stable. In the center was Ozma, her arms encircling the waists of Dorothy and Betsy, who stood on either side of her. Ozma was nearly half a head taller than the two other girls, who were almost of one size. Unobserved, they had listened to the talk of the animals, which was a very strange experience indeed to little Betsy Bobbin.

"You foolish beasts!" exclaimed the Ruler of Oz, in a gentle but chiding tone of voice. "Why should you fight to defend us, who are all three loving friends and in no sense rivals? Answer me!" she continued, as they bowed their heads sheepishly.

"I have the right to express my opinion, your Highness," pleaded the Lion.

"And so have the others," replied Ozma. "I am glad you and the Hungry Tiger love Dorothy best, for she was your first friend and companion. Also I am pleased that my Sawhorse loves me best, for together we have endured both joy and sorrow. Hank has proved his faith and loyalty by defending his own little mistress; and so you are all right in one way, but wrong in another. Our Land of Oz is a Land of Love, and here friendship outranks every other quality. Unless you can all be friends, you cannot retain our love."

They accepted this rebuke very meekly.

"All right," said the Sawhorse, quite cheerfully; "shake hoofs, friend Mule."

Hank touched his hoof to that of the wooden horse.

"Let us be friends and rub noses," said the Tiger. So Hank modestly rubbed noses with the big beast.

The Lion merely nodded and said, as he crouched before the mule:

"Any friend of a friend of our beloved Ruler is a friend of the Cowardly Lion. That seems to cover your case. If ever you need help or advice, friend Hank, call on me."

"Why, this is as it should be," said Ozma, highly pleased

to see them so fully reconciled. Then she turned to her companions: "Come, my dears, let us resume our walk."

As they turned away Betsy said wonderingly:

"Do all the animals in Oz talk as we do?"

"Almost all," answered Dorothy. "There's a Yellow Hen here, and she can talk, and so can her chickens; and there's a Pink Kitten upstairs in my room who talks very nicely; but I've a little fuzzy black dog, named Toto, who has been with me in Oz a long time, and he's never said a single word but 'Bow-wow!' "

"Do you know why?" asked Ozma.

"Why, he's a Kansas dog; so I s'pose he's different from these fairy animals," replied Dorothy.

"Hank isn't a fairy animal, any more than Toto," said Ozma, "yet as soon as he came under the spell of our fairy-land he found he could talk. It was the same way with Bill-ina, the Yellow Hen whom you brought here at one time. The same spell has affected Toto, I assure you; but he's a wise little dog and while he knows everything that is said to him he prefers not to talk."

"Goodness me!" exclaimed Dorothy. "I never s'pected Toto was fooling me all this time." Then she drew a small silver whistle from her pocket and blew a shrill note upon it. A moment later there was a sound of scurrying footsteps, and a shaggy black dog came running up the path.

Dorothy knelt down before him and shaking her finger just above his nose she said:

"Toto, haven't I always been good to you?"

Toto looked up at her with his bright black eyes and wagged his tail.

"Bow-wow!" he said, and Betsy knew at once that meant yes, as well as Dorothy and Ozma knew it, for there was no mistaking the tone of Toto's voice.

"That's a dog answer," said Dorothy. "How would you like it, Toto, if I said nothing to you but 'bow-wow'?"

Toto's tail was wagging furiously now, but otherwise he was silent.

"Really, Dorothy," said Betsy, "he can talk with his bark and his tail just as well as we can. Don't you understand such dog language?"

"Of course I do," replied Dorothy. "But Toto's got to be more sociable. See here, sir!" she continued, addressing the dog, "I've just learned, for the first time, that you can say words—if you want to. Don't you want to, Toto?"

"Woof!" said Toto, and that meant "no."

"Not just one word, Toto, to prove you're as good as any other animal in Oz?"

"Woof!"

"Just one word, Toto—and then you may run away."

He looked at her steadily a moment.

Chapter Twenty-Five

"All right. Here I go!" he said, and darted away as swift as an arrow.

Dorothy clapped her hands in delight, while Betsy and Ozma both laughed heartily at her pleasure and the success of her experiment. Arm in arm they sauntered away through the beautiful gardens of the palace, where magnificent flowers bloomed in abundance and fountains shot their silvery sprays far into the air. And by and by, as they turned a corner, they came upon Shaggy Man and his brother, who were seated together upon a golden bench.

The two arose to bow respectfully as the Ruler of Oz approached them.

"How are you enjoying our Land of Oz?" Ozma asked the stranger.

"I am very happy here, Your Highness," replied Shaggy's brother. "Also I am very grateful to you for permitting me to live in this delightful place."

"You must thank Shaggy for that," said Ozma. "Being his brother, I have made you welcome here."

"When you know Brother better," said Shaggy earnestly, "you will be glad he has become one of your loyal subjects. I am just getting acquainted with him myself, and I find much in his character to admire."

Leaving the brothers, Ozma and the girls continued their walk. Presently Betsy exclaimed:

"Shaggy's brother can't ever be as happy in Oz as *I* am. Do you know, Dorothy, I didn't believe any girl could ever have such a good time—*anywhere*—as I'm having now?"

"I know," answered Dorothy. "I've felt that way myself, lots of times."

"I wish," continued Betsy, dreamily, "that every little girl in the world could live in the Land of Oz; and every little boy, too!"

Ozma laughed at this.

"It is quite fortunate for us, Betsy, that your wish cannot be granted," said she, "for all that army of girls and boys would crowd us so that we would have to move away."

"Yes," agreed Betsy, after a little thought, "I guess that's true."

THE
END

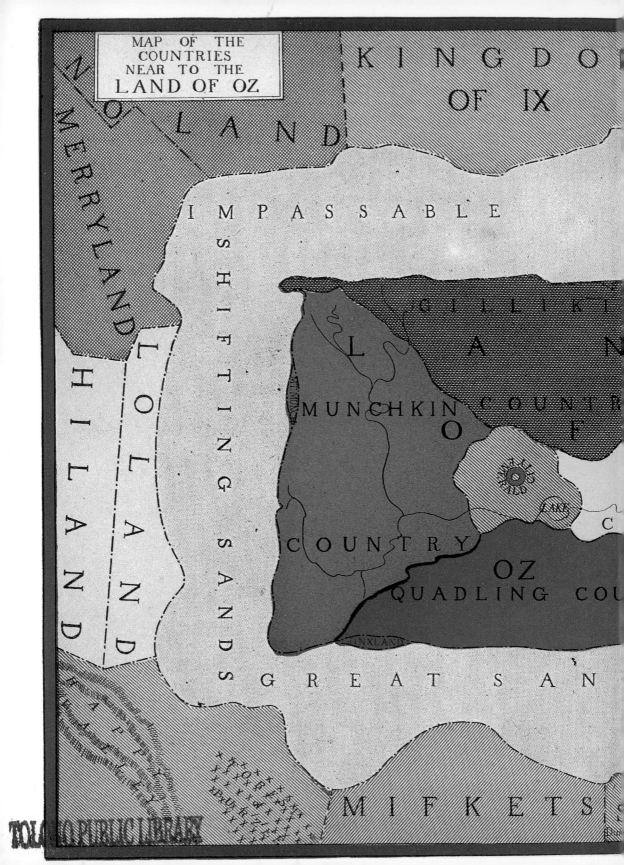

MAP OF THE
COUNTRIES
NEAR TO THE
LAND OF OZ